Beyond Unconditional Love

© 2024 Marlies van den Broek
Publisher: BoD · Books on Demand GmbH,
In de Tarpen 42, 22848 Norderstedt
Printed by: Libri Plureos GmbH,
Friedensallee 273, 22763 Hamburg
ISBN: 978-3-7597-9422-2

Written by Marlies van den Broek, compiled by Marlies. Beyond Unconditional Love is a rebranded love story. The best released in 2022-century. The best of the early twenties and before with over 10 years being unpublished until this publication in the 20s century. Now that it has been published and shared it has been passionately rebranded and compiled with the writing by really beautiful people in helping her and find sources of her manuscript. Special thanks to all who helped. She loves to know that fabulous people loved reading this last edition fantasy romance thriller and for readers to mention the parts they enjoyed reading.

Beyond Unconditional Love

A story from the heart

By Marlies van den Broek

Beyond Unconditional Love

Love Story

In a civilization she didn't belong, among humans she never knew, she found a way to make a difference between her sparkling passion of enchanting beauty, love and cursing divine. The cocaine rage in their veins, nose bleeds and their hearts are going to burst. The story is about L, the beauty queen and S the clever manly well fit, cursed handsome divine, both wunderkind who came to their defense.

"A wolf can survive in 30 days without vampire tear but the moon and 3 days without transformation nor a heart."

Part 1

The sex was untamed. The longing for
these touches has grown towards each
other after a long time of being apart.
And this while S gives L everything
that her heart wants. It started with a
dinner. A blind date. A meeting later
it turned into sex. Real powerful,
tender sex. This time with strings
attached. A love agreement. Sex is
what both were craving for. And that
it may have turned to be the most
wild and exciting touch. It was
immense that all possible of luxury
came at hand. The sauna, the Jacuzzi.
It was their honeymoon. After taking
a shower she choose to wear red
lingerie out of her suitcase. She
covered herself in a black kimono. L
looked herself in the mirror. The
lavish appearance of the cloths she
picked made her feel elegant,
admitting that this outfit raised her
thrill for that moment. She sat herself

in front of the mirror to do her make-up and 1 gram of cocaine. He would arrive in a moment in suite. "You look dazzling my beauty queen" he says with his manly voice. S, he greeted L with a kiss. She smelled his aftershave. There was some delicately music in the background and on the salon table there laid a mirror with cocaine and nearby the couch a cooler wherein the champagne laid cooling with two glasses. "L, you smell delicious while still human" he sighs. "I'm yours now. Do whatever you want to with me, I won't abandon you for every touch." She replied. S kneeled in front of her and gave her kisses with his soft lips while he grabbed her boobs and gently gripped them. She closed her eyes to feel his kissing movements even more in her thoughts. Than S removed her breasts out of her bra and located her boobs as far as possible in his mouth. With a wet, and soft tongue he licked her lips between her legs. Just before L is about to come he stopped. He stood up to undress himself. He was fast. He didn't use a condom this time to pull over a banana or his stiff penis. He aimed his penis into her pussy. He entered his penis all the way in his length inside of her until she could feel his balls. First gently, but after, the hits became faster and powerful. L her vagina cramped, her clit throbbed, her pussy tingled and she moaned at her highest point. At the same point she heard her man of her dreams moan too. He filled her fully while moaning. After the change they gifted themselves under the rainy shower outside in the rain and they stroked each other with a bird feather on the twin bed. After both their highest point, they dressed themselves and they finished the night with a game of chess and cocaine.

Traveling to different worlds brought different lives and different belongings alongside every trip and a curse fantastically persevered. Some places were packed with divines and others less. The wolves from Amsterdam liked to play. Especially with the demonic burglars and vamps from Acid Paris outside Dorthrin Firegale into the deepest and darkest era's of hell no one wants to end up in, also known as hell. They wanted to play an addictive original somewhat sex French cards game for 8 up to 20 players. The crowd, they have been divided into two groups, the humanly burglars and a tiny group of wolves. The game was lead by natural persons and has been played during day and night. At night the wolves would eat innocent burglars, during day citizens of the village had to be carefully to recognize a vampire to offer the wolves. As a revenge for them to be burned. The city of Amsterdam was packed with wolves, as did a tiny group in Paris. Once was developed by *Pallières* en *Hervé Marly*.

The captivated lady L lived in a splendid small village with fields long enough to hold shrubbery Dandelions. This is where L and S, the clever and charming emperor wolf, spent their time. Lying down with heads pointed to one another on the grass fields while S would blow this lovely flower on her enchanted face. Dandelions originated from severe continents like Oculus Star Way, Tree Nebula World and Droplet Cloud and by the love of him and her they were glowingly spread over these entire continents from Dorthrin Firegale. The ones they knew are to be blown away in the name of politeness and true love. To be honest, nobody knows which one of the three is the one she and he actually carry during their way towards the avenue. The flower

Dandelion is what he and she loved. They would always remember this glooming golden magical flower…

Time passes by in the cold winter days and splendid L wishes to no longer take part of the civilian world known as society. L has wishful brilliant memories of how it would be and holds a *Babylon Candle* wishing for her change. Time would only pass quick no matter where she would heavenly go even if it were to close a deal with hell somewhat darker than Dorthin Firegale, just to hold the moment of a movement with change in heart and soul. The way demonic humans are sometimes although they aren't animals like birds it is hard to grasp for a girl like L. With wishful luck she let them go in her soul but the strains and throbbing will always remain in her heart and nightmares. She had one sparkling crush that came and left that she treasured forever in her memories, S. There was something silly about the chemistry she will always remember. There was some kind of madness through the darkness that felt cold and warm, no matter how hard or soft. She created a relation with him. They were connected in her dreams. It felt like an imprint or something she longed for in him. That time in the winter felt like glowing diamonds with fire, sometime courteous blooming in wilderness, sometimes freezing in the cold with elegance. L shall never forget the bliss and pain of demonic citizens. Once the sun arisen and the high tide of the sea reached, he was gone and the sun would set. This was the end of L her sinful and malevolent memories as a human with Crown moon.

Shrubberies were magically glooming in the most prettiest colorful sparks. Especially blue dandelions and black roses with Bordeaux red thorns. S and L knew that these flowers where magical. The flower became a symbol of honey love and once mingled politely the symbol would turn into eternal love. During the passing time, he and she would wait to remember the fields when they were young. Both fantastic young divinities of spirits among a few clever and talented beasts from Dorthrin Firegale.

Later as beasts in life S and L wondered if they belonged in Dorthrin Firegale. In their hearts while they did everything about it to fill in the empty peaces of their wondering feelings in the lightest fires of hell. L turned into the same kind as S because she wanted more to life than a human. She wanted a purpose in life as an enchanted wolf married to a wolf emperor, a place to belong in Dorthrin Firegale, a world somewhat different than the human world of civilization among society, demons and bad people. He is her home. She knew from the moment she met him, that day so many years ago at the train station while heading for work when she was still a citizen. Now her fire is burning for her Halflings. Half human and half divine children. L gave birth to twins before her change, while she was still human and S was a wolf, something empirical. Life shall always be filled with joyful sounds of un-emptiness while their Halfling son and daughter practice their homework and practice their guitar and piano between two worlds, in Dorthrin Firegale and in the human world as undercover citizens between humanity and as fantastic whizzing Halfling beasts…

It was forsaken moon and it was hunting season. The children resisted longer days without transformation, even by diminishing moon, nor a

heart. Some weeks turned into
months, years turned into seasons that
clever S and splendid L resisted some
time apart before having the children
to feed magical milk. After birth L her
gifted change took place in the
strongest wolf that ever came to an
existence due to their marriage, her
enchanting elegance and supremacy.
Both were insanely falling in love and
for trying to find each other while
both weren't aware of one another's
crush-love but both were wishing that
their enchanting hearts were heard.
After the change seasons went by and
there has never been any distance
between them ever since and there
never would be. Some eras before the
change she tried reaching for him in a
silly and madly way wishing he was
staring at her from the outside at the
same forsaken moon and into the
corridors of her new apartment.
Wishing he will grab the keys that lay
under the doormat or, ring that

doorbell and he comes running into the living room to tell her how stupid she was for being so silly about the way she behaved so insecurely by the love of someone else's way of giving. L went to sleep with S his picture every night to feel some kind of armor during her beauty sleep as a human, he has always been with her, his charms, his smile, his courageous, his preserving. L hearts S, S hearts L. Both heart one another…

Part 2

Once they grew up to become wolves in Dorthrin Firegale, somewhat close to the darkest fires of hell, she was seen as a wolf daughter of *Medusa* and he was seen as a wolf son of *Lucifer*. She became the beast of love, female enchanting beauty and fertility belonging to one of the many other foremost pretty beasts in Dorthrin Firegale. She was loved among different creatures, shrubbery and animals. The loving of other female beasts found she origins in the East and found her magical way to the center of the world close to a new continent.

There are different stories concerning the birth of the *Medusa* prophesy raised enchanted wolf beast of love. After have being dressed in spring season clothing, the wolf daughter of *Medusa* was sent to take a part of the demonic game and became immortal.

If she would change she would become an empirical immortal wolf that cannot be touched nor killed by anyone on planet, earth nor caught by wind, water. Except for firebombs from the deepest fire from earth and hell. Atomic bombs that beep before they explode.

L, with *Medusa* as her godmother fairy, she was the enchanted beauty, the growth of nature in spring, the *femme fatal* and the pleasure of loving deeds. She would seduce her demon vampire victims, mostly manly vampires demons, with her enchanted beauty and by sleeping with them by game. By spending one night with them the damage would be done. Their blood would be infected with her venom and their bodies and heartless souls would be eaten and torn like a beast. She had her beauty. Even the son of *Lucifer* noticed, S. He was a war wolf and both gave birth to twin children. The children became like the birdie love Halflings and raised by divinity and in Dorthrin Firegale hell, by godfather Lucifer and godmother Medusa.

In Dorthrin Firegale, besides S his engagement with his niece, female cousin wolf, he could leave his special romances in love and passion with others. S is a wolf known as a war wolf. Ruler over Hell and Earth, as a son from a father of divinity and consumer of demon vampires. When on the planet he landed in 3 tops, in a village not to warm, not to cold and as a beast. He won the battle against his greatest fear. He lived among humans in the mountains in Droplet Cloud for 19 years in his humanly form. He got married with L by Crown moon and created his beloved Halfling son and daughter with her during their honeymoon night. He, S, was the wolf of war and was lead by his heavenly leader Lucifer, the protector of right and moral, of state, housing and empire and guests. After S, while being an adult, defeated the demonic villains and felons, he grew his absolute power and became the ruler of all. The intelligent emperor wolf. He became the wolf of light, thunder and lightning. S is the believer of the people and leader of the wolf empire its power.

S lived high in the mountains alongside with other animals, shrubbery, creatures, beasts and they where recognized as champions. Although he was married to his sister he always had a weakness for other female exquisiteness. S was the last son and child from the mastermind saint marriage in Dorthrin Firegale from hell. Through history his father had the power to resist longer than 3 days without change nor a heart and to survive less than 30 days with vampire tear including the diminishing moon and gave him, S, full consent to continue and collect the supremacy. His father envisioned that also he, S, would be more successful with this power by marrying of Medusa her daughter. He took measures for the necessary or unnecessary and fed her with placenta of their children after birth. Only S and L had the smartest *Liszt* song from their parents.

Before getting married or engaged in a fantastic settlement, L and S had to accept that as magnificent fiancé and fiancée they could have made more magical children than expected that both decided to keep both child as a secret from birth. He and she and their children were raised in a family village from hell in Dorthrin Firegale. In the villages of Dorthrin Firegale beasts, creatures and shrubberies lived in village *Superbia, Avaritia, Luxuria,*

Invidia, Gula, Ira, Acedia. They could travel through 3 star villages tops and if more where crossed the darkest fires of hell could interfere and get hold of the animals and plants and suck them directly to hell. S and L, their ex's were once confronted with the gates of hell and luckily sent to return to their homeland in the human world and took with them the gemstones that were meant for S and L. The stones were sealed with a message to be given as a gift to the one. At that time the one were their ex's. They ate it before even looking at it. In the years after. S became courageous, confident, gorgeous and strong and decided to visit his father after becoming a grown up optimistic beast. After the Crown moon and have given birth to their Halfling daughter and son. He and she were proud to introduce their two children that both families are blessed with to have given birth to.

Emperor S had a relationship with his first love, L, and they wanted children. L became pregnant during their Crown moon. This was before the transformation of L into a stunning beast by her charming wolf. As one of their best friend forever, happened to be a female cousin that gave birth to a full-blooded wolf. L had to hurry with the change into a wolf because she was too alive while carrying two children in her tummy. She gave birth to empirical beasty twins. One of the twins would be a mastermind of hunting and the diminishing moon. A pregnant girl who never married and decided to stay a virgin. The other twin would turn out to be a brilliance of light and music. She was the genie of the Sagittarius. He was the genie of animals and shrubbery.

Gifted L was the beauty queen of the land in Droplet Cloud and as a

Droplet Cloudian wife she defended her ruler wolf S to the utmost. With her king she gave birth to divine children. Both she and her children formed the brightest stars from the galaxy of Dorthrin Firegale like twins and belonged to one of the most important talented elite.

Bright L was the eldest in the family and had her fame thankful by her beauty and shyness that could be seen from all daughters. After being charmed by S. S was the first son that later became the divinity of crows, dogs, and thieves. She sleeps. He dreams. Both stargazing. Both are sharp about the importance of love, beauty, sexuality and balance, as talented elite. Both families had one boy. One boy was born by romance with love.

Through the years humanly artists tried to compete in striving to illustrate the beauty of L what in turn

made her one of the most famous
classic mystic wolf. S was a son of
Nightmare. His attribute was a
thunder lightning elegance. He did
have many truly long relations, with
immortal girls and wolves and mortal
girls, and he wished to create
countless of children. To make sure
his wife is being lead around the
garden he transformed himself as a
crow when he gives himself into the
path of tenderness. He wished for a
child to learn *Latin*. Being brave in
school and amazing in after-classes
activities. Their child would be a
talented one known as a Halfling. S
would plan to lay their child on their
chest once the child is sleeping. Until
every drop of supernatural milk
spilled formed a new continent. There
were other who did everything in
their power to destroy the love
between S and L. Sadly, others
included civil children whom mother
was not famous.

Part 3

During the nights of forsaken moon glasses of red wine poured on to alleviate the thirst for burglars and demonic vampire blood. He S, and she L, alone choose to be beyond the bright moon for both of them to be in the comfort of their unconditional love as just magically married beasts imprinting their sex on one another. A beasty affection to never leave hold of their witnesses. Their waters run wishing to not see one another in another's arms. Not in touchiest neither in sight. Both heads want thrilling love as has been magically spread by shrubbery blue Dandelions, their torment souls warms them against worship, known about past jealousies and tears, in order to still have strength for their soul to still love. The love, even as their unconditional hearts keeps on forewarning them. Love makes their blighting magical hell hearts strong and keeps their heart on both feet on the grounds without flying away. Both have bird wings too! Both kiss, both eyes dazzle and get lost whilst giving them their look and kiss. During civilization when S was an undercover wolf and L was not aware of his un-civilization she wondered: "Shall I poison him with my kiss?" The one. During that night, before the change ever was seen to come into existing, he kept filling both cups mingling in thoughtless conversations while pouring the wine. The one wine with that sweet name made S admit about his blissful and divine powers and his curse. Drenching with both scents to remember. Both sent those roses for both to look, to be more than friendly and lovingly, the coverage of tears because both where elsewhere and not here. At night during their honeymoon was the moment L became captivated by the change into a beast with family powers too.

The divine curse of both S and L was to do something with music. The outrageous music both made had the right magical touch. Both wanted to escape together yet they didn't. Their genius hearts surrounds both and together they wish to give both a chance to breath for their muse upon them with their desire of divine beauty their way. Both stay up and awake for the un-famous. They would rather hear each other's sweet whisper and the piano of acoustic guitar in their ears.

Crowning their shrubbery magical flower, their Dandelion and black roses. Their flowers that bloom violet with the winter and fall bringing wishes to their Crown moon love, to be loving in the rain, in the fields of marriage by their darling equalizers. With the remembering of "I love you my love", said by the fantastic bride and groom.

They wished to be prepared to meet the might of jealous hands. Knowing both still lay awake and wait, unsleeping to not forget who loves them with guidance by the animal owls and lions with no rival to make them jealous. By dawn.

She and he are in a great fire ripe for love at their deadly 33 possessing every charming and greatness, and their kissing lips of honey, a most perfect enchantment. A beautiful fulfilling love, what can they do to make time go fast forward, to allow them to do more than looking only. Both feel erupted apart, shed by tears, both want it all or nothing at all. Both had a magical magnificent pale skin they liked, also the color of the face like honey, then again, their black hair and everything beautifully enchanting about them keeps them going, and not to forget the playfulness of their big brown eyebrows. Both must admit that together they are over the top. The letters 'A' and 'E' in their names have the same numerical value, which both found out by chance that in Ancient add up the same sum: two. A simple kiss and a letter

The more S touched L the less insecure she became and the better S became. The evening was thrilling. The two beauties became ripe for love. They wouldn't abandon each other. Both had the dream of having children and wondered how they would turn out to be. Also the dream of getting married. "I Do". L giving S her honeyed passion without embellishment. Both had a prayer to feast upon. After Acid Paris outside Dorthrin Firegale… Both beloved ones. After the marriage, if they get married, they shall always stay together and never apart and shall the pleasure of yesterday succeed to please another again today. A simple love. If today were pleasing the next day would be even more pleasurable was the outcome.

During S his imprint he showed L that they are each others *Amour* and *Sauvage*. *Mi Bella* and *sauvage* are mostly the words S uses to commune with L, they never disappeared taking off from their bed on their own. Love should not be considered dangerous to all hearts as neither Sky, nor Earth, nor Sea, Medusa and Lucifer shall admit the known grandfather of their children. It is so strange that love shoots fire arrows in Dorthrin Firegale on laughter with looks. After all, love is not only marriage. The sword and heart equally share in marriage. The same stars, and bright moon that light the way of beasty lovers. Staying at home as charmed prisoners. These wishes of love offered by evil to them.

With the imprint both pray and talk together, *mon amour*, *mi* Bella, went to sleep into their sleepless passion for their love, my love. Both give and have a voice that would leave words even if one of them got killed.

Both had love and likeness of the wolf pack for the love they gave to their boy and girl. Both souls lost it and found it. To have a place of worship of love imprinted in their soul, they would stand even in kneeling before Mother and Father for the thought not to be jealous and learn compassion. Both have tasted the soul sweet honey. Both have kissed most beautiful young man and young woman, their lips liberated. Both kissed.

Everything for the lonely beasty honey-loving beasts named by him, and she were taken to heart by dropping honey from his lips when he sweetly kisses. The animals took their beauties pleasant passionately with a good heart to be followed by demonic vampires and other demons selective eyes and fall, looking beautiful enough to inflame each wolfs heart like fire. Both can be skinny but sweet with not much between them, rubbing flat on her breasts and feeling his heart. Like the Forsaken Moon, it's light and outshines the countless stars. Loving each other is best for certain kind of female and male who take relationships seriously. He teaches her the cursing cure for that mad lovesickness. Now neither poor nor rich in love with fine cure has hunger for a Crown moon while pretending he is from down to earth. He has a big thing in succeeding in getting her to lay with him, their hearts were pounding, surprisingly he and she are in act of secret lovers. Now overheard as wolves and no longer a secret but it is the talk of the town in Dorthrin Firegale by the animals, shrubbery and creatures. Their beasty behavior was fantastically gorgeous with no force.

One more night to go before the special month of *Augustus* arises. This is the splendid Golden-month of their love and that of the bright moon. During this month the wolf emperor enchants young women in misery with his graceful lips, love from his heart, and music from his hands. He captures with animal bird songs in their heart. So conceivable in allowing S to satisfy L, even in her dreams and nightmares when she was still a citizen, she bit him with her *Bordeaux red* poisoning lips by excuse. This only harms humans but not S. "Please, my love do not hurt my heart. If shoot you must, try for some other part." Both go after golden love, with winter fresh violin flowers. Gold turns out to be experience for getting their love. Imprinted wolf dreams lead them to whispers and hearing of tomorrow. Clever wolves like S give their lover what they can give, for lovely L it is as a gift of a broken promise.

Wishfully married is right where they left and wish to begin again, but now magically Gold-crowned, falling nervous in their mind like the wind through trees overcoming with the beasty buoyant passion for him, and again love excites her, magically invincible. In brilliance deathless ways while weaving outrageous children. His original Queen and her clever King. Don't let them inflict her further with heartache and the beautiful sparrow of wings from above, delivered from heaven. Blessed one with a smile on their deathless face. She wanted more than anything for her manic enchanting heart to lead back into his love. Both will love magically. Again, release her from unloving sorrows and all that her heart longs to fulfill, fulfill both, and may he him-alone be hers. Soon both will look ancient in glooming golden garden-lands of flowers bringing water, wine and roses. Lucky he sticks around, turning her on for a thousand years. As a witness she called upon a brother who is known with her wish, acknowledging them to have 4 adopted children and two children of their own with the hope for a twin. She has done S no wrong against him, he is her husband, her love, and let it be justified by the eyes of their Preacher, and let her be seen as a loving wife and a devoted mother. This coming month, unforgotten, is splendid pricelessly sealed.

Part 4

L, her parents and grandparents were highly gifted, heavenly brilliant and masterminded. Many of these were recognized as blissful divine. The worship of them is with overwhelming achievements. Outside Dorthrin Firegale, Acid America was discovered by someone who actually made mistakes. *Columbus* was an adventurer, who was a heavenly blissful. *Gauss* was exceptionally gifted, many don't even know him. *Einstein* is more famous than *Max Planck*, because his theory brought the audience to a much more masterminded surprise. *Joan of Arc* and *Giordano Bruno* have their worship as a genius, because they died at stake. The mastermind is also referred to as madness, and indeed. The public seems to look at geniuses as abnormal insane appearances. The fame of a genius is actually strange and visa-versa, surrounded by an amazing atmosphere of the divine, conceived by the tendencies in its cursed clever soul.

In art there are abundant of heavenly masterminds. The painter *van Gogh*, who lived near Droplet Cloud are samples of their madness. Talent on the other hand is developed. Talent is ability. L and her enchanting cleverness prince, S, were really talented and their performance involved capabilities that gave them a natural gift and curse, in a limited setting. Their curse was to live as "musical talented lovers". Highly gifted is more general, because the natural talented gift lies on the bias of intelligence, they go on until the level they no longer reach higher than first place and start to get thirst and heartless. It is like two fools in love computing miracles. The whizz society named the "creatures, animals

and plants morons". Friends of him
and her were also referred to as
"creature morons". They were
actually calculation wonders.

The brightest change of L was her
talent in drawing, painting, theater,
music, magic, sport and languages.
Her father was talented in music. L
her prince was talented in everything
just like she was that was caused by
the change of his venom. He
performed in a perfect way. They both
resided on creativity. They are
developed in a high level of intellect,
coupled with a development of
imagination, creativity and energy.

He told L that he was a shy wolf but
that was one of the highly gifted
competencies. He was social in the
pack. He accepts other beasts as they
are, accepting mistakes, is interested
in the world and galaxy, in time by
forsaken moon, has social
consciousness, thinks before speaking

or acting, exhibits curiosity, does not judge, evaluates precisely the relevance of the information that is available about a problem, is sensitive to the needs and desires if others, is sincere and honest. He was magically charmed.

Part 5

The wedding was planned with crown moon for the coming winter of December 2012 on a Wednesday the 12th. It was a day to always remember. In L her dreams she couldn't wait to feel S her manly hood and his bravery that he would come walking on two legs instead as a beast with four feet with full confidence towards her while she was still a civilian. Their wedding would be surrounded by the presence of human paparazzi and animals and creatures in their most humanly form except for the shrubberies. The shrubberies would be present as their decorations in the cold winter magical golden glooming enchantment. It would be the time of their Crown moon night. The night with both the Crown moon and the Forsaken moon in the right stand for the golden night to get pregnant and the change. It was no longer a dream but originally December the 12th in 2012 and S could hear L her presentable heart, smell her scent and feel her audacity. To celebrate this era, the wedding party was filled with champagne and delicious dishes, all really festive in a winter wonderland. Medusa and Lucifer both attended the wedding too from a distance without the humans noticing. After both said "I do", both believed in the luck of the bride and groom to sparkle over the years for their optimistic future. After attending the church before of the wedding an animal in its humanly form caught the flowers outside church of the bride before the bride and groom entered the *F-type* to drive to the wedding party that was held in an enchanted winter wonderland. It was an action of good luck in the mystic world of Dorthrin Firegale. Once an animal of that kind catches the flowers of the bride from an emperor wolf it would be the next for marrying. Before leaving to their enchanting crowned moony destiny they got to open the thrilling dance floor with their first dance together. It was the dance to always remember like *Guns 'n Roses*. There was a woman on cocaine, who they never knew would be at the wedding, she accidently bumped in during the wedding into their dance performance until they fell off their feet on the dance floor almost hitting a table were a pack of wolves sat with the danger to let them expose themselves… the woman came to reveal the cursed secret of S and she didn't care to reveal her own curse towards the human paparazzi that would spread the news on *Fox news*, she took a bottle of champagne and interrupted the wedding by complaining about the quality of the cocaine she was given… It was *Carmilla*, a demonic creature…

Estries de Adze Nachzehrer its body might be dead but the soul remains on Earth. These creatures and demons are obsessed by the thought that its physical body has to be saved. Saved from unbinding from death. It feeds itself with human bodies from victims. Victims of the city, their blood disease does not let them live in daylight. Parts of their body die when showing themselves into daylight like fingers. Many stories have been told in big cities. It is a disease passed on by demonic parents that exhibited this in the past within these small areas. That they survive on others blood. Demonic vampires from Acid London. A blood transfusion on regular bias. Also the stories about ignoring them with your own defense. A demon shall do anything in its power to ignore the break off. Everything extra to the victim results in gain of body parts.

The demonic vampires are oversensitive to sunlight caused by transformation in their DNA. Not being produced well enough resulting in a mass quantity in their red blood cells. The red blood cells are in turn partial of blood. They transfer oxygen to body organs. It mainly transports itself to skin and sometimes organs like liver. To travel through daylight they have special suites attached to the skin, absorbing sunlight. The skin first becomes red, swollen, itchy and painful and burns.

Oversensitive to sunlight and on the long term failure and damaging.

Varney the demonic vampire and *Carmilla* the female demon from *Joseph Sheridan Le Fanu*. There is no clear image about their looks, characters and skills in their strengths and weaknesses. Everyone gives them their own twist and turns, because everywhere in the world they have and created their own presentation. A mostly known figure of older generations. They mostly sleep during daylight, they grow old slower than humans, physically they become ten years older than people and the aging starts from the moment they choose to live the life they currently live. If they cannot feed themselves on blood, the blood sucking cursed demonic animals become much older than the people or other creatures from Dorthrin Firegale.

Having extra long teeth and hunt lost souls in big cities just like Acid London, Acid Paris, Acid Milan, Acid Hong Kong, Acid Singapore and even Acid New York recognizes their appearance. Sometimes they principally look like normal humans, apart from their features, the pale skin and maybe a somewhat skeleton facial appearance. They need blood from humans and enchanted beasts to stay vital. With preference of human blood. Carmilla, she is always thirsty but can stay away from blood when necessary. She is a leader of the French card game pack. The looks differ strongly on the story of the city. He or she is sexual appealing, dresses in black and has an unnatural pale skin.

There are different ways for undergoing the change to become one of them. One myth is to be bitten by one and for you to die and later rise from death and relive as one of them. If we had to believe this fable it shall consequence that the entire world should be overloaded with them, because of every bite would result in a newborn. In many and current stories there is a newborn. The only way it comes to existence is if the bitten one drinks the blood of the one that bitten it. Blood exchanges itself and makes the transformation complete. Slightly a small part of the people that is changed by a bite becomes one of them. The others. The others simply die by one bite or don't survive the bite and eventually don't become a newborn. Power. They do have above natural powers like cursed wolves do, such as muscles, great speed, a tremendously good hearing, a good nose, enormously fast, make someone believe what she wants, change in appearance in mist and sometimes have the power to manipulate the weather. They rather prefer cloudy than sunny. For the rest they have outstanding manipulative gifts and not to forget great beauty. Also the power to command fellows under the same roof during night. These powers are meant to mislead her puppets and over rule him or her. In many stories they can fly, also without having to transform in mist. They are mostly extremely adaptable and can make very high jumps. Their powers can vary per movie or myth. Weaknesses. They do have weaknesses. They have something against wolves and wolf packs and enchanting beauty. Demons, they are continuously afraid of the cross and holy water of the Lord *Jesus Christ* and other religion symbols. One of them can only enter ones home if they are invited to enter their place. Once invited demonic creatures can enter the house whenever they want and there is nothing that can stop them from entering. They start feeding themselves when invited into your place and once invited they decide whenever to come and visit and market the place. Once in a while a card is sent or a package of your favorite odor or movie reflecting your human personal life.

Demons. They do make some exemptions but mostly live indoors during the day, because they disguise the daylight. Showing themselves into daylight weakens them and in the long-term this can lead to their destruction. Sunlight wakens them only. For this reason they prefer only to live and get out at night, only if necessary demons will show themselves during daylight if it is a high cause. The taught of sunlight as their destruction has only remained a myth and currently a mainly acceptable brand of theirs. This has been seen at first in *Nosferatu*, and in *Symphonie des Grauens*. Some use and engagement ring or wedding ring and name it a day-ring to avoid the sunlight.

According to wolves in Dorthrin Firegale fire-camp stories told in the forest they cant leave alone to count everything that comes along in their path, and can in turn be misled by spreading something on their path. Besides they have a hard time with crossing streaming water. They need help from others.

To love demonic vampires you need to make drastic changes. The most known method is a silver ring, like a one-style spring needle right through their heart. During fire camping the stories told that she needed to be nailed on the floor, but in movies it is more appreciated to drill through her with a battery operating boyfriend long and strong enough most of the times. Other ways are by killing, whether after her mouth has been filled with blood, and burning her up to the dust of her body or nothing. This once was a drcam of S and L.

Part 6

"Give me screw or nails instead." Said the Lord, *Jesus*, about nails. L was hit by the use of another objective creature the animal, which made L stuck on the second objective creature the beast She could have been separated by means of another object, but that will mean that they are no longer together. There is the strange legendary marvel that, although a nail itself also can be called an objective beast, it cannot be attached in any other nail, at least not with the objective animals as described in techniques and tools. L her modest beginning was invented by wolf Franz the grandfather of Lucifer. He had lived. In Droplet Cloud, the same origin as she was. It was on the second path to left in the woods. Franz came with the idea when he at first bought a hammer. Unfortunately he didn't know how to use it, but he knew that it once was bought and discovered by a humanly king. The king tried to hang a painting on the wall with it. That was the point that the road of useless hammer went to a functional hammer with nails.

The development of Franz was devastating. He creeped in the cellar of his studio that was created by civilians. That he put so much effort in his work, that he even could see the roman invasion of the time and letters without any notice. When he at first invented a prototype of the nail, the development in Droplet Cloud drastically changed. As a divinity he didn't limit himself to technology. Instead he worked on his inventions immediately and told the story to the village. Due to technology, they hacked Franz and her granddaughter L, via their phone due to the creative invention. So Franz decided to go back to his cellar in his studio, switched off all devises and kept working on his creation. His new version was splendid and smart, and the romans used it to hit the holy man on a cross. The decency was a major step of improvement.

The nail Franz had invented was as a killer to society directly from hell. It had led to many murders. Thinking of The Lord Jesus that at his century was hanged on the cross with nails. Other nail murders are *Will Smith* and *Pim Fortuyn*. He used to be an extremist politician in Droplet Cloud. Moreover, there is a long time that nails are not in high water. At least, that people think, because there are rarely golden nails in, let alone gold to low water are found. Nails are heavier than water, even heavier than heavy water. But until nails are found on high water continues to be searched.

Life would be sad if there is only one type of nail. Golden nails or bullets were a danger to divines of Dorthrin Firegale . Through the centuries there have been creative's that did not only realize it was a great invention, but also did something about it. A few of the creative created the nail in the warm late summer. A widow named *Maria* whom was married to *Willem*. *Willem* was killed in a battle. The widow, *Maria,* now had to survive from a pension that consisted of convenient shining coins. She accepted this from her husband. She didn't know what to start with the large quantity of coins that her husband had left her, and she decided to try a variant of the ancient nail model, even a bullet. She was of the opinion that the longer and thinner the nail, the thicker the wood could be combined. This rather than the traditional nail that was small and thick. It became famous and they named the nail to Maria. She became so famous that they even made a sculpture saying: "We Thank Thou Widow Franz. Thou Made Us A Needle Richer." Franz van den Broek. He died at the age of 35 from the same cause, a bite from both a wolf and an *Estries de Adze Nachzehrer*. During his empirical search for love.

Struggle and struggles she has tried quitting the spread of her venom and stay away harming demons, burglars and vampires. She risen up and had a fall back in tasting blood. Each time she was using she did this to forget her nightmares. Her first love and she wrote each other letters in their younger years. She needed food and a pair of new clothes. How had she come to this point in her life. She used to be sharp with well-dressed fancy clothes, severe cars and smoke *Vogue*. Now her fingers are yellow from the tobacco that she rolled 14 a day in her working chair or laying on the couch thinking of how she fucked it up this

time. All bodies are revenges from her
dreams. She had been stuck in cocaine
for almost one decade now. She
decided to make a New Year
resolution to quite drugs and
consuming demon blood but they
keep haunting her. Some of them
returned in a cursed animal, evil
spirits from the deepest fires of Hell
outside Dorthrin Firegale. They came
by night, when she was actually
supposed to sleep. She quite, she quite
and this time she will keep the
strength to stay away from them, but
how can she possibly try to begin a
new life with S when she is stuck in
the same site. She would need to re-
locate into a new house that she can
call her home that she can decorate
with new furniture. For now, an
apartment is good enough for her
with a balcony. It would be nice if she
was here. Her BFF's, true family and
true friends. These include humans
and animals. Creatures and

shrubbery. Them knowing of the change. L, She is now his and both can have polite sex now without someone getting hurt. That she is his honey and he tells her that she is a Beauty Queen including his Bella. She needed to quite pale facing herself and maybe these voices outside her apartment at the first floor might have gone away. This was the place where she hid her victims. She heard guns shooting and fireworks and she believed they were meant for her, but they were not. Today she didn't touch cocaine and it was weekend, the demonic villains didn't call her and she didn't have their phone numbers. The burglar dealer, drug dealer, murderers and junkies. All belonged to her list of victims to eat or spread the venom and tear their hearts out. Most of them belonged to the demons or vampire animal pack. She is proud for so far. The last time she consumed vampire blood was two weeks ago on a Friday.

She took sleeping pills at seven in the morning after having used 4 gram of cocaine and her heart stops beating fast after consuming their blood. She takes XTC-pills to make the cursed voices by the demon bite disappear and sleeping pills because she lays awake at night with her eyes wide open thirsty for more demonic animal blood. Her beasty husband, wolf, first love and king broke her heart during outrageous and rough sex. She had no clue of how to react. She couldn't sit and look him proper in the eye. He asked her "do you want to have children". At that moment all she ever wanted was screaming for ice.

In the human earth, before the change she fell. She fell in-love with him over and over again. At the first day she regularly saw him entering the train in the same station. This was before she knew that he was a ruler wolf from a different earth.

Her ex was attached to her and other guys who could have ruined the relationship between L and S. Both thought this through. She, L, even asked him, S, to get engaged via *Meta*. But he simply refused her request because of her ex and he went on with his life. She was in pain and waiting in vain. Until she met him again after a couple of years. He had a relationship after both dated and had sex. She moved on with her muscle been torn into pieces and she lasted down on the couch to recover for one year. After one month of devoted love she disappeared from her apartment. She told her father she was in love by enchantment, wants to get married, that she wants to be engaged first and that she wants to have kids. After one week S visited her apartment he held her newly changeable by captivating wolf beastly hostage. She thought he would leave her, but he was still in imprinting her head. The more she hears him speak is the more she loves him. The imprint worked. Both are thrillingly in love again. The guy who broke her in pieces. She thought she couldn't write a page but she was already on to another page of writings to him about the love story of her life. She didn't feel like going outside and felt even more uncomfortable in her apartment without the present of a wolf, him. It is almost going to be cold. She bought herself some nice pair of leggings. White ones that match perfectly with her white and black dresses. She doesn't crave for cocaine. Tomorrow she has to do a urine test where they check if she has been consuming cocaine or weed or even worse a combination of the two including XTC-pills and other pills.

During her time as a human, she had severe weird nightmares. One of them was about her cousin and her friends. They where trying to help her. She wanted to find out what the nightmare actually meant but she couldn't find any decent source to help her with the meaning of her dream. She started her new job yesterday and it was fun and a little bit strange at the same time. When she is at work or even visiting her younger sister for a BBQ she doesn't hear him but feels his presents. He surely imprinted on her resiliently with his manly hood. Only when she is alone in the apartment unless someone comes to visit her she can feel his present. No one does feel lonely but can be alone for some reason. Waking up this morning and thinking of the dream she had last night. She was seeking solutions to her day-to-day activities. Some routine. Some distraction. Giving advice to her boss on how she can improve her current peace of work that she has been working on in editing. L her cousin helped her to

create a URL for her *Google* account.
Her first love helped her to use her
money wisely. She sometimes had
situations that her neighbors, who live
in the same flat like her came to visit
her at night and use cocaine at her
place, but she refused to join them.
They stayed a bit and one of then
went paranoia and had to take more
and listen to specific music. They told
her they heard from the streets that
she was using so they insisted
beforehand that she would join them.
She told them that she left drugs long
time ago and that she was working on
her personal life. Her love life.

This morning she woke up screaming
her cousin male, his name. Guess she
missed him a lot. Since the separation
and before that, they never got a
chance to grow up together. They
were having a family meeting at her
place and everyone was insisting she
was fantastic and that they were

worried about her condition because she was really originally social. Especially her father had his opinion that she was bizarre but she didn't feel diligent at all. So she told him to take her to rehab and ask them to return her once she comes clean…

In the past she volunteered to go to rehab, but she was not qualified enough to join the AA-meetings. She would need to be a stronger consumer of liquor, cocaine and other stuff. So everyone of her family decided to leave her place except for her cousin and his boyfriend and brother. They actually found her place really awesome and chilling with the music she was playing. So her aunts and uncles, fathers, mothers and younger sisters and brothers left her place and the some others stayed. She offered them an ashtray and somewhat music they would like to listen to and they chilled and had fun talking about their younger years when they were together. Family was gone along time ago. Even more *raison d'être* for the change.

The hollowness of his love worked the first time both saw each other that they knew it was true love that both would love one another for forever, and that's what they'll do. He doesn't have a clue what he does to her, her looking at him. She made a promise with her heart. Today and always. Beyond tomorrow. She needs him besides her, always as her best friend and forever lover. He is her unconditional lover and they are miles apart from one another, but their souls are connected, and she always believes that the flame of their love will burn forever in hell or heaven. His kiss is sweeter than strawberries. His love is increasingly beautiful with a bed of black roses with thorns. His touch is like a mountain. His voice makes her and the birds sing in the morning. She would be so proud if he would choose her to spend a lifetime forever with. She loves the sun, the moon and him.

In humanly form, she had another troublesome nightmare and sleepless night last night. Well she had a dream about her neighbor living on the top floor. He is a burglar and a thieve only striking at night while humans sleep they say. Before falling asleep she could hear him screaming loudly with his fellows and by night around three to *4 AM* it all of a sudden stops. She changed her name of her apartment and covered the window with a scarf and she had this funny dream that he was trying to break into her apartment and he kept peaking and jumping to see if she was sleeping on the couch. She thought she woke up with nothing left in her apartment except her bed. Little did she know did the wolf place a dream catcher in her bedroom in a secure place to prevent nightmares from occurring any longer until she would be changed into an enchanted wolverine. While she would sleep this catcher would read her picture book and they would be close to her by the comfort of her thoughts. It felt like magic.

She believes of her wolf that whenever she was cycling next to his house that he would be hiding for her but they were sort of playing hide and seek and whenever they caught each other they would smile towards one another. So sweet. He named her his *senorita*. He came to her in her sleep. He told her, the rebound chick, that he didn't love her, and that he was waiting for L to come because he missed her so much. L was so frightened that he didn't love her. She had to think twice what to tell him. So she decided to hurt his feeling too by telling him that she was waiting for her manager to come and do her. He ran away.

"*Jesus* of God. God almighty. Please let him love me." Is what both preached. Last night she believed that he would watch over her while she was asleep. But it is just impossible. Lately she thought he was watching over her from outside the window. Her love for him is so much, that she created an imaginary character of him. He was so great, or is? There is a difference. She just loves him. She is really shy and doesn't know what to say to his voice. One day he wants her and says she is his and the other day he says "no!". She thought he was really standing there and he keeps showing up in her dreams. She guessed she is just a fool in love.

She will try to keep reaching him. How her heart gets toned. He is telling her to wait, but she doesn't know if she can wait any longer. Both used to play table tennis, swim and slow dance together, both used to sleep together when both were young. He was her first love. Her loved one. She thought she saw him standing there outside the window. How he made her life complete. She means, come on, he was standing there with a white shirt painted in black. How much she would have liked to take a picture of him just standing there. Oh his love, he misses her and wishes she dine. He tells her to wake up and then he disappears.

She believes that one day both will make it. But what if both make it without one another and decide to come back together, she loves him. Yes. S, her wolf but she curses him at the same time. She doesn't know that he actually already is cursed. She just wishes she could trust him and be there for him as much as she wants

him to be here for her. She still hears
his imprinted voice but she cannot see
him and she sees signs but she doesn't
know where they are heading to. This
is love. For real. Both are their one and
only. She believes he was there. In the
room. Yes. The room where the party
was. She wearing her beautiful blue
dress and that her stepsister and her
again new boyfriend, after abortion,
were laughing at her. She ran away.
Away in the forest with forsaken
moon and she spread her wings. She
had a dream about her family. She
slept really long, but what she has
seen during the night is just
something that can't be replaced. Her
stepsister who is pregnant and her
cousin. To start with her stepsister.
She is currently pregnant and at night
L saw her crying out loud after 18
months of pregnancy. She had a
broken arm. L could see the blood of
the baby pumping in a picture
perspective. L asked her what

happened? And she told her that her current new boyfriend beat her. So L, she took a bamboo stick and followed this guy and put him on his knees and beat his bear skin back and ass with the stick. L insisted she took an abortion but it was too late, and she kicked him after he was crying and wounded with blue spots and marks on his back and spit on his wounded body. The dream about her male cousin. They were at a party. I do not know if this is related to the thoughts of L thinking about her female cousin, his sisters wedding, but her cousin and she were finally connected together with their uncle. At the party L was lost. Nothing is what it seems.

Cheers! It was time to celebrate a yearly returning event, L her Birthday. During this sole day the most expensive wine bottles like "*Las Pueretas*" vino de Chile, were poured and all champagnes went to merry.

The humans used to say that her father didn't have a spine and that she was a rotten apple from the inside and sparkling from the outside. L her sister and friends were according to the crowed empty headed with no attitude nor character. After the change we could only laugh about those tubeless souls and pour our expensive drinks over their civilian heads. S was an ancient wolf. He would actually step towards her father to ask for her hand. This is something that her ex's didn't do. Before the slow dance during their wedding L went through a memorizing episode with her ex where she was threatened and almost saw the light. Reason enough to chose for an early enchanting change. Before the magical imprint from S, during the wonder winters she would breath in snowflakes. Her magnificent bones could be seen by everyone. She barely weighed 25 kilos at the age of fantastic

20. She was so outrageously unhappy and everyone could tell. She smelled like death. Death caused by the civil-war-cigarettes she smoked alongside other deadly poisons. The winter jacket was warm enough to pull her through the coming winter of that era. L was a true enchanted beauty. Beautiful enough to let go. Let go of her ex who kept her underfed due to shooting, screaming's and sometimes she wondered why he beat her up. She was a Mulat from the Oculus Star Way continent. By the time she graduated from university she showed to be thinner than an average western human girl coming from the East of her age. Most of the western girls would exercise daily to have her figure. Teachers, students, whoever was in her circle were shocked when they saw L. the human girl with the winter jacket and the red scarf. She was so magnificently thin that her bones came out of her chest, as if her

aorta could give up, and way beyond norms of a healthy adolescent. Little did they know that she could look an eagle in the eye without the eagle trying to move or eat her eyes out. According to the eagle she was already written to death, death was all around her scent. For L to be more willing to be changed by S.

Students started to actually interfere. They were curious about her dinner. She was so hungry. Hungry enough to be capable of preparing chicken in the microwave. L was honest, she wanted to be honest about her cooking that she didn't cook. Back at her apartment she was a pile of bones in a house of shit due to the open sour right outside her front yard. Unless you live in the open sours in third worlds, there is none student in the entire world following university that is dealing with the same problem. Not one. L was different. She was so rich and poor and left in starvation by her ex that during daylight she would eat her own lips because she didn't feed herself with enough meat.

The imaginary tutor wanted to know why? So he started reading the letter L sent him and made notes for himself. He figured out at the end of his summery from the notes he took that L, from Droplet Cloud needed a lending hand and was searching for a reason how come she struggled with personal conditions. With luck the foundation had a more positive spine to the problem. She was simply unhappy and immature enough to live alongside someone who isn't supporting her with love. All she needed was love upon death. Earth, wind, air, fire and some TLC. So her plans for her wedding in December the 12th got interrupted because someone within the circle of eminence knew she found love of her life.

Someone, may it be human or some animal must have been following her on the digital platforms like they did with Franz with no good intentions.

The vampire Carmilla was sent by purpose to change L on her wedding day. Before this time, S was abounding and fully aware by his hollowing curse lead by his ancient wisdom, godly courageous enough and with ruling charms he had one darn ironic manly hood wakefulness.

Part 7

The name of a magical lady and magical gentleman has a legendary reminder of a playful time where the Titan creatures where being converted to Christianization goddesses and genies in Acid Europe. The existing name at that time, in the age of true fantastic divines was "*Freyafugle*" an animal bird from the goddess *Freya*. A roman to our loving ladybird and loving gentleman bird. The first change lives ahead in Acid Germany outside Dorthrin Firegale that later arrived in Dorthrin Firegale in distinctively form.

They have many possible drawings, ranging from glooming orange to almost sparkling black, but the creatures revenges are recognized upon their black "S" shape drawing. The most magical colorful third world lady. Aggressive carnivore. Their Oculus Star Wayn weakness is like

Rwanda Hotel. Other magical ladies, cocoons and butterflies can threaten the indigenous lovers in Dorthrin Firegale.

The genius divine creature families were close to the life of ladybirds. They are appearances like enchanting Cleopatra. Some well known. Similar to the spotted animal lady and gentle-bird. The ladies are magnificently strong. Their classes are of small fantastic elites and mostly seen as valuable winged animals, birds. Ladies have gentlemen that are ordinarily happy fleeted that are alike to the tall whisker with a blouse to cover the neck shield. Drawings. They adore glooming red, white, black and orange color. Mostly magical dots. The enchanting babies become carnivores with a vegan diet that are mostly protected by aunts due to their sweet personality.

Once the restraints arise towards the animal ladybirds and the gentle birds and there is a sign that S and L are being tortured by pressure. Wrists of legs became a magical malevolent sense and released bitter taste after smoking tobacco. A magical bleeding reflex with enough blood to kill if sometimes left alone for their feathers to fall.

The red and black tone glooming patterns of the creatures are declared as a warning. Their poisoning and filth taste escalation appears by their strong craving also known as longing. The nasty taste is caused by smoking or drinking that depends on the consumer.

Oculus Star Way ladies animals are used for the battle in a natural manner to destroy outrageously. The most colorful third world country ladies. One of the main reason for introducing the western specie, in both the most fantastic colorfully western gentle and third world country ladies.

Before they made arrangements to get engaged, married and create Halflings. She, L and he, S had a childish life with one darn bond in the world of animal birds, shrubbery's including trees and beasty creatures. Besides this they wanted to start a family. A new home, a new ride and a loving network. Humans and demons surrounding L and S carried diseases and worldwide recognized danger that could infect beasts too like atomic bombs, measles, Ebola, Corona, all sorts of bloody diseases that they knew, with or without a cure. Some of them could cause death upon all of them. To protect their Halflings from these terrifying diseases and bombs they needed to be magically charmed by the Destine Prophet Palm tree. Both received a bag filled with cash, enough for the Halflings to travel and stand alone on both feet within both worlds that of humanity and Dorthrin Firagale. Both, L and S, made sure that no matter what that the lives of their children would be secured. They could go to school, have their own home, could create their own habitat if something would happen to L and S. These thoughtful decisions have been brought from down under, by the wisdom directly from hell's village Superbia. The humans, their ex's, once known left them alone. During festive celebrations like memorable moments like birth dates S and L were being left alone including demonic vampires although they somewhat interrupted their daily activities. For both to ignore them and to not invite them into their newly daylife. Both were untouchables and astonished.

L and S were in a point in life were they had to reunite somehow after parting for each other and with family after the magical change. The beasts wanted this to happen soon enough. Either by meeting each other coincidently or through relatives, one way or the other, they were meant for one another. Both screamed, sighed, cursed, shouted and persevered many nights to their village of their kind and the beasty pack cheered!

Humans would make bounty jokes about L and it went like: "What's a black hooker filled with cum?". In return for this favor the wolf pack created the monkey joke by bewitching the humans. Each time if a civilian girl or boy would insult L, or harm her, they would buy a banana during daylight and by night they would follow the girl or boy and put a condom around the banana and penetrate with it in those who found the bounty joke funny. Once they are finished and the banana got cursedly stuck they would throw the girl or boy away like trash with laughter. The ruler wolf would just hand over the banana and peal and consume it while watching while the other wolves of the pack penetrate the bananas into the humans. The girls and boys would come begging for more while the banana was still stuck but they would have to see a Prophet Palm tree in order to remove the banana condom that got stuck. It was an act by the companions of a wolf pack. The Prophety Palm tree would ask if they understood the monkey joke. A bounty chocolate remains white on the inside and dark brown on the outside and this doesn't count for a Mulat. She is such an enchanted beauty without chocolate. It was simply dark enough for those to not recognize all of them.

In contrast to L during night. She would look towards herself in the mirror and put on some make-up, get ready and get dressed in silk. She would be wearing her ballet colored blue dress during daylight with the most expensive pearls during night that match her white dress perfectly. She would be cycling, rowing, walking or driving back home before 12 o'clock, at midnight, so that she wouldn't notice the crying of the wolves with forsaken moon. It is always a month, year or season to never forget. He, S, who asked L to slow dance with him. While they were dancing he even asked her for her hand and if she wanted to have children. What's a lifetime without a child life? Their wedding and Crown moon. She will always remember… The perfect flawless time, where she changed into the man his nature that happened to be the ruler beats of wolves she didn't know he existed for her to live instead of thinking of ways to die.

She would imagine a *Grand* teddy
bear like the one she kept near her bed
stand, underneath the *Eifel Tower* of
Acid Paris during a wild with
demons. Other nights instead of
thinking of ways to die. The optimistic
avenue that lasted during some night.
In a magical evening, like not many
other nights, L would dream of her
true love like the shrubbery
Dandelions spread themselves by the
wind. Whenever she reached to his
sexy imprint. He would be touching
her until she howled with sweat all
over her body and especially her
stomach like shrubbery flowers
blooming with spring ready to bloom.
Her abs tightened after every tense
abs movement like the uncovering of
the flower. So intense that she wanted
to scratch his back with her fingernails
to let him know how much she liked it
as a Dandelion shrubbery wanting to
spread its seed into the galaxy by the
wind. No further than her hands on

the side of his buttocks she wants to feel him moving up and down outrageously making love to her like a spider wanting to spin his web around its territory. He has an excellent masculine shape and he hits her with every movement so that she reaches her climax like a enchanted spelling animal bee hitting every letter of the beast its beat in the right reading letters of spring. She's a bit playful but can't go anywhere with him it's like a shrubbery trap of a sand castle transformed into a sandy village with seaweed appointed as a villages roof. He makes her sweat from every abdominal muscle he tightly gives her and it only lasts a moment. That moment was all night, in her forestry dream alongside with their shrubberies.

Part 8

Their ancient years when they were younger where witnessed by the eyes of Lucifer. What happened earlier to him and her was ordinary but less frequently in other continents. The most famous pedophile, he whom escalated the story about the beauty L, who was sixteen at that time, insisted that she was playing her game against the law. He actually warned the girl beforehand, but she didn't have a clue. So before he caught and the night before he put his dick into her. He watched a scary movie. He said: "shall we watch a movie together?" and he showed her a movie named 13. It was 16 minus 3 years her age. It was an awful movie but sixteen, L, was not afraid of it. She loved it, except things started to make sense after that night. The movie was somewhat pedophilic about a teenage girl who was kept hostage in a cellar who was told to sleep on a mattress on the bare naked floor and was jelled at to come and eat oat meal tightened up on a chair. Whenever she puke she was forced to go back to the mattress on the floor and eat again after penis succession, and after successful growth she was released on the streets with bruises all over her body.

"Knock, knock, knock" said the door of sixteen. L, she opened the door. He was standing there with a gift and kissed her immediately with his spelling lips on her lips. He walked himself in the house. "The man" the man whom so called saved her from wisdom, courage and bluff. He pointed at the Persian carpet. It wasn't even red or beige. If you asked women if they wanted to have sex with him, the 45 man, 30 percent would say 'yes?' and the other percentage would say 'no!'. ADELEW from the poison he gave her in bed named WELEDA. It was massage oil that he used to massage sixteen her back and that of other younger girls thoroughly including their lips and to figure out how the texture is of the girls' hips for precision of the first breakthrough.

He was not really the type of man that would lay a banana skin hidden behind a pillar to let a passenger pass by and fall flat on his face… Or blow up a frog. She would have done the same to him. He wouldn't have organized a terroristic ramp in eye with his proposal. He wrote his story to the personal on two A4 papers. Far across and beyond the borders. Whereas the average population would say he did it his way. The point is he didn't have deeper thoughts. There had to be and come something new. Like the interactions that existed between *social media* platforms within groups and other 'IT' applications from the firm. Via *Whatsapp* from *Meta*, groups the population could easily take care of an old lady who was sick at that time. The family and sixteen, L, needed to take hand of this opportunity without having society taking care of these conversations. The letter was beautiful she wrote. And L, 16, she pressed "send".

There used to be a family drama in the boulevard. That it concerned a family drama was revealed by the police. Someone told them that there was a family drama that took place and that it was a place of hell. It was a tragedy. She committed suicide. The case could have been limitcd to the news if a tragedy. Forty five, a man who commits a hopeful and painful act to a girl.

There were fast conclusions and speculations via social media and *Whatsapp*. it was sentimental. No deeper motive from the man than

ordinary curiosity in her that all of a
sudden put himself in the storm of
media. He was a fast talking man
without a sense of explanation. The
family decided to leave the drama the
way it was. A drama. Between a girl
and a man. By means of deleting him
out of their lives the family could take
distance from this man and restart
their lives.

Is the man the sheep we are looking
for with five legs. One dick, two arms,
and two legs. In his previous life he
was searching for other young girls
including his daughter to penetrate
his masterpiece into their pussy.

On the hard drive of the government
there is an illegal system downloaded
named "Good day, to die Hard". Well
she found it so hard, that she decided
it was time to wait his turn. He was
downloading files from other people's
computers to gain profit without
paying for other people's work. The

45 *"whistle-blower"*. He was being maneuvered. The man, whom was an illiterate on his highest level of education, got caught.

"Gas weapon", "*l'arme de gaz*". It appeared several times in technology about the story of him and her, but seldom sparingly. She preferred "energy weapon" like described in *Foreign Policy*. But there was some uncertainty about the conflict between him and her. There is need of time to look at the development before it could have been evaluated later. It was war. With war there is no need of snoopers. The snoopers might think that they are the only one that have the power of an energy weapon, but she could also trigger the gas weapon. Is there actually a gas weapon? It was a wind farm to grab the energy to save the girls from him. Thou shalt not invite your father to meet me or I will break you.

She cried all night long. Her crying under the shower could wake the entire city together because of her throbbing. She was hurt devastatingly.

The first thing she did in the morning was walk on bare foot in her nightgown, she heard her neighbors turning on the television on *MTV*-music while she turned on the radio onto her favorite channel and lit a cigarette. She heard the neighbors play all of her songs that she used to play in a remix before she got damaged. This was even more hurting than the event itself that took place the night before. L Smoked outside the window. The neighbors didn't love it. A cigarette by sunrise. A cigarette with coffee. She was tremendously unhappy, she could barely catch some sleep and had sex. While listening to the radio the news mentioned to have found many mistreated and dead bodies of boys and girls. The journalist mentioned something about animal and beasty activities. By this report S came into the picture. He traveled through the entire universe of love sent by Lucifer to find L here.

After a couple of days with sparkling thoughts L awakened. This all happened during a visit to the café that she mostly visited in the morning before going to work to grab her espresso or cappuccino each and every single morning realizing that the one she should be with is the one she meets during the week at the train station when she heads for work. She had a plan. She decided to move. To move and start over again with mister right S. With or without him only unknowing of his true origin. She took an international flight first to pull things together moneywise.

Spending her last drop of money on her international stay at the "La Royal

Smile Hotel" she found a decent piano to play on. She played on a black winged piano in the hotel hall. She felt miserable and played the most magnificent saddest *Chopin* melody and hopeful tone than ever before. A joyful melody and a more thoughtful one. L was playing this after figuring out that her first love that she was in love with is perhaps her true one and a divinity from hell but couldn't figure out from which layer of the two from Hell. After, she went to take a long bath with bubbles and a cigarette with wine to think about inflicting the change on herself…

Part 9

The journey of The Lord *Jesus Christ*. Before the Christians used to be a man who was a shepherd named *Dumanzi*. Yesterday it was Good Friday. The day where the population rethought that The Lord *Jesus Christ* was crucified. The day before it was white Thursday. It is a mystical enchanting story. This because of L pledging sins for The Lord almighty to make the decision to kill herself. The pain of *Jesus Christ* was thought to her when she was young. It teaches those who believe to question things about life. A real beautiful story. *Dumanzi* also seemed to have risen from his death. Just like the God Mithras and other more than human, genies and divines. You don't have to be a Christian to believe in Easter. Growth, hope and a mother freaking middle finger to death.

Kings day. L thinks of her ruler wolf. He is her king when both get married. He is relaxed and chill and always happy and looks outside the window and sees the evil demons from the darkest side of hell. Light and darkness is also in the study of nature. The golden crowned prince turned into an animally frog due to stress and pain and wanted to be kissed by his original princess.

The king almighty wrote a letter to the rehab. He wrote: "Dear youth AA-meetings, you want to see my fiancée. You say you want to see the growth, behavior and system of my enchanting beautiful fiancée. At home we do not have the impression that there is something wrong with the three beauties, but if there is an outsider who wants to view our point in life, well well well. Ok than! You also want to know if we, as parents, have any dysfunction in our health as parents!?" Well all her parents could say as Lucifer and Medusa and other hell wicked beasts, animals and creatures is that they believe that the relationships between them and the hall of eminence is limited that we do not want to share intimate details about our voices. Later a couple of years she and her parents decided to invite the demonic *watchers* to her house and share the information via digital conference. They felt uncomfortable. They wanted to know if she brushed her teeth, how many meals she took a day, how many in between meals, fruit, vegetables, milk products and fish and meat she ate. The differentiated trees from the Prophet Destinies Palm trees informed her parents if she, as a child used to take swimming classes, did any sports, if she was rested in the mornings or even if she peed in bed at night. It was a shrubbery war between trees of different forests, the white forrest and the grau forrest.

If the development role behind each other, and every analysis needs to be adjust. The news doesn't go faster than in the past. She was being confronted with unknown places that within days transformed in Acid Antwerp and Acid Brussels.

45, the man threatened her in 2012. He wanted L, sixteen, to give the disk where all the company information was stored. He was crueler than once before. With his longer hair, black eyes and wearing glasses. Lucifer and Medusa suggested to him that they would rather fly than hand him over the work L created without defaults that he messed up. He was surprised. He was totally surprised. L and S were in that time unique divines and were not fooled by idiots. Why did the affair appear now and not before? Back in the time she would have known better that it wasn't a perfect coincidence. It was a joke with lots of truth hidden. At this point, Lucifer and Medusa were a bit further in the case. At work he, the pedophile 45 didn't want to admit and shout out loud that he was wrong and that she, L was right. Instead he came by night and pointed out her mistakes. L and S were cursed hero's who fought for freedom.

The death assault and for her to commit suicide was all over his website. According to the letter she wrote and the book she read by *Paulo Coelho* before she committed suicide he suspected at her stay ate the "La Royal Smile Hotel" he said he was an innocent man. In the meanwhile he committed crimes by abusing his two-year-old daughter. L, 16 and her prince, S, they both died in their later years because of their change. They were no longer seen as humans and died after their wedding during their Crown moon. The masterpiece of people like him who bring thoughts to younger children confirm principles of soul to soul are of the opinion that they act like this in a really planned way. But what man like him don't know is that when she decided to commit suicide her first phone call before she jumped in front of the train was to the man to tell him to check whether he has *AIDS*. That was the moment the man didn't believe in God anymore and went to the hospital to get an injection. It was like the "*The rate of False Conviction of Criminal Defendants Who are Sentenced to Death.*" It is a conservative estimation of what she thought before the train was coming. The problem and pain of the innocence was much larger than the thought. All of a sudden after her death there was an instinct of chemical solutions for the deadly injections. The family killed by means of injections the man who killed her and his daughter. In the mean time, before the dawn came, there were two executions placed and planned on family members.

More and more desperate. A long while before execution. Every innocent person who commits suicide makes the system go crazy. All of a sudden there are the wizards from out of this world of humanity. The wizards from University, but that is how it goes. In all University's around the world are wizards that seemed to be related to spirits of searching for evidence about who were correct yes or no. The man was sentenced to death. The wizards already had the correspondent and they held an interview with him. The innovation of technology and system hacking of the illusion had not come to an end yet, but it was simply a pause on its way to a bigger war. There will be and come more pauses, but before dawn the train station whistle was blowing for another committed suicide.

Thoughtfulness occasions. The days seem like acts before the TV-episode from 1946. It seems like a nuclear proof but actually it is simply an ordinary attack with an atomic bomb on the girls with oil named WELEDA. The sheep and other materials are being brought to the ships that are going to paradise while the oil WELEDA. The 45 year old man, 45, also referred to as a pedophile used it as a law on toilet paper, that thou shalt save 30 percent. He had creepy thoughts and he was of the opinion that there are enough beautiful enchanted humans let alone unknown creatures, animals and shrubberies to destroy on this planet. Those who walk by his side, in the finance world, will not be haunted. The family of the 16, L, were just hoping that the procedure in harmony court would soon come to an end.

The working class battle is nowadays corrupt. Especially for female in the finance world,. The so called loyal leader, the man, is being adored, with his mean tong or dice also known as "Game of Dice". He stayed on the workplace about the family's daughter that she was deliciously cheap and malleable. Well there are more people that gave trouble shooting a job. But this was it? He was just as a dog that is attached to his boss, and stays faithful to the remaining leader. He is going to the end of times in the benches to play for his new victim. Downhill side of heaven, from falling until he becomes a dictator. A danger of young divine and enchanted beautiful girls starting at the age of 2.

So after all it is not such a logical plan. To smile in the life and nature or what ever is left of it. What we need is a master plan of mobility with train, car and bicycle to avoid such man and to stay anonymous. The traveling paradise for all girls and women.

When L was sixteen, she received the greetings of the supervisor from her internship in University. The supervisor sent him to do it with 200$ tip. The message returned and sent from 16 was about many families and about many other stuff. Conclusions.

They took naked pictures of her. All off sudden they told her that they where on the *Internet*. So she checked the web. It happened to be that the pictures were edited of someone else's body and her face, just like *face-in-hole*. Her friends from Acid London came to save her. She traveled through time machine to her friends in Acid London outside Dorthrin Firegale and they showed her what was going on. She could not see. No one told her.

They took her devices and connected them to an antivirus system and the photo's were deleted. She traveled back to time with an airplane and talked with her magical animal and beasty friend to tell her that she was receiving *e-mails* about her wanting to know if she was a sex girl behind camera. The plane had an accident and crashed. But luckily a man could save her. Who that man was, no one knows. Once arrived at home, they burned the house down where her family lived.

Now 16, L lives from social security. Not a really bad one. It is a law of retake. The basic level for Dutch to come in the social security system is F1. You are supposed to speak basic language such as "What are you coming to do?", they said "I want social security". This was followed by the guidance, and assessment and grading of the social security that would shortly be a science in itself.

It was an international flight that lasted 12 hours to get her to "La Royal Smile Hotel". The destination was comparable to the same journey since 1996. She had everything arranged. She had a driver, keys were reserved at the hotel and very sightseeing arrangements were made as soon as she felt ready to undertake the activities at site. For now all she wanted was to enjoy the new world and the ocean. Nearby the ocean there was an island that could be visited by a speedboat. All her savings where invested into this trip knowing that everything would be different by the time she would return. The environment she was in was waterless causing the water in the lake to decrease tremendously. The lake served for multiple purposes some for fishing, other inserted pipes to transport water to households for bathing and other purposes. The thoughts and memories of home bring her to realize how poor she actually was in her love life and that she was in constant war against a love that was never meant to be. She had to leave that home this instant. She has walked for miles to find her one and only love but all of them where running fireless and couldn't add earth or wind to her love. When evaluating her home it was clear that she needed space. To many broken hearts and to little space. She was held hostage at the hotel that was perfect for a while because of Corona. Corona was the most actual danger known by animals and human population. Many people died. She wanted to commit suicide in her hotel room while running the bath full of water. Isolate and drown herself. At this time with no vaccine nor pill against Corona, death was everywhere.

Out of quarantine she called the driver of her limousine who spoke fluent *Latin*. The driver drove her to her favorite restaurants at destiny and he talked with her about beasts from Dorthrin Firegale. This was the first time she learned about shrubbery trees, animal birds and all sorts of creatures, beasts and heaven and hell and most importantly about the severe levels of the two. One can have 1, 2 or more sins and go to hell but one surely goes directly to hell once committing suicide or kills someone. By knowing this L, she went to do some research about heaven, the earthly heaven of missionaries from the White Mothers and the White Fathers. They blessed her and warned her to have been born luckily captivated and that someone who was from heaven and has fallen bringing life to earth from hell has stolen her soul before the eyes of evil death. She felt pain, pain of un-acceptance by the doors of heaven, pain that death is hungry for her soul. The heavenly missionaries consisted of a dazzling team that wasn't pretentious and arrogant or with too much ego. They gave L a tour in their sacred running schools and holy sanatorium that were created and ruled by heaven while she was still a human. L her thoughts needed to be distracted constantly because without it she would be stuck in thoughts of S. Now she understands why he's extremely shy... Now she understands why he is tremendously talented... Now she understands why he is.., He is a divinity, cursed… he is a wolf… Not an original gentleman but one clever beast and a ruler of all wolves…

During her stay in her new world at the "La Royal Smile Hotel" she rethought the situation of the eagle that she held on her left arm. Her questioning goes on and on in her mind. How come the eagle didn't eat her eyes out? Most animal birds that eat humans don't wait if you look them straight in their eyes and attack the human until the civilians death and share the dead body with other creatures from Dorthrin Firegale that resist from human flesh. Animal birds feed themselves on humans that are almost dying from starvation. She was in bad condition after all, but she could have been at her worst. Why all the others and not her. The puzzle started to fall in place. Something was about to happen if she were to return from her international trip back to Droplet Cloud.

Part 10

After 45 laid his hands and eyes upon L. Her prince arrives and saves her. He who was so proud of her enchanted beauty, but yet so insecure, made a mockingbird animal sing the song in early spring and summer that she and her prince could sing along. She and he had young and old lovers flocking at their door, but nothing ever seemed to work for both of them. He offered her a mirror, since she could not bear the sight of her version in the mirror due to the loss of her virginity.

He was a magnificent skinny love and oh so sweet. Unfortunately there was not much between them, 45 and sixteen, L her love for him, S, still exists and every time she sees him she keeps falling for her prince charming. On her flat chest she lies on his heart.

She has prayed for one night with him, to fulfill his desire for a mad boy's love. She said: "Now that I have your sweet body next to me, I am spent, all tuckered out and drowsy." A full desire.

After 2 years in 2010 they meet again and he asked her: "What happened to you?" she told him that he was not so lucky that day.

She was poised for fight, afraid of heights it would ruin over parents, lovers, a keen riding over truth and detail.

She thought growing up would be the rising from everything. Together old and earthly, not these faltering steps out the door every day, then back again.

She came back from her daily walk through the forest and saw a fantastic miracle. More and more people are beginning to see them straight on and for longer periods of time. The explanation we get from skeptics and marvel is that it is nothing more than the active human imagination. Whereas their apparitions are almost always a misty white, vaporous or have a decidedly human form and appearance, whereas shadows beings are much darker and more shadow like. It was her third eye.

Her inner eye provides perception beyond ordinary sights, the gate that leads to spaces of higher consciousness having deeply personal spirituals associated with the ability to observe love including out of body experience. "She had the mind of *Christ*"

Her prince and friends where some kind of smokers. It was good stuff. Hell yeah. It seemed like it was *Sensation White* instead of the finals. Smoking is not new. It belongs to football. It came along with the ball. An invisible ball out of history. There was much to be done for something. '*Apocalypse* Now' said the prince. It was a great history at the ball. The wedding party after the wedding. The ball.

When the prince saved her there were a couple of deaths. Just like '*Sweeny Todd*'. The prince told the man "lay down you motherfucker, on the ground you fucking pedophiles, do not make a move and sound, and hope the wind and storm runs over you without any name damage!". In the first phase he told him nothing would happen. In the second phase that there is a slight chance that something would happen to 45, but that it would be wise for the prince to do nothing about it. In phase four, there were more deaths than any possible man could imagine to save her, and that all possible lines were overwritten. Phase one.

Long time ago the prince and L, 16, wrote each other letters via water. Putting the letters they wrote with their own handwriting in bottles so it could travel safely through oceans. Bottle mail from a different universe. The letters where written by the prince whom was 8 and 16, L, was seven. At night in bed he wrote with the right palm of his hand on skins of paper his secretly *Wolver Hampton* crying in Latin. The next morning he would insert the letters in the glassed bottles. He cycled all the way to "Sealand" to leave the bottles in the ocean and wishing they would arrive to 16, seven at that time. After having pleaded his prison ship after pilling the man the prince decided to leave to Acid Dubai, not a real working paradise. The nice thing about the letters is that they make a much larger impression than worries. But what the hack. We all know this kind of love story. He could have always say "it wasn't me!".

What do we have on a better world than tomorrow, if you lose your daughter or son today? Prince was always available and invested in other countries. He was a shelter. He could live with the death of 45. It is not all so one dimensional in life. That a torn father, because of the death of his sons and daughters, was against the humanity that resulted in his death. Lost children were not only about 16 but also about 2, and the son of an artist. His son fell. He was senselessly offered in front of the altar with lies, delusions and opaque needs. But the humanity will be described later as soon as the children are killed.

Her prince started to appear more and more in newspapers around the continents. Especially Acid France and outside Dorthrin Firegale to Germany. He was back again in the spotlight. He thought that the past was the past, but this was not the case. 22 bombs, 9 deaths and 130 wounded fell. Ten children had been hit-by-hit man 45. Later involved in the awful war, which was not supposed to be talked about, but after it had passed by into history and would be made public. She said: "*Herres* out of grave!" and she spit on 45 his grave. Finally peace, peace at last. The Good Friday agreement in April 1996. The wedding ball history in 2012 is the time. The time that the family reunites again. A 21 year old organized the wedding. The prince and L, 16 were like glimmering twins. Both went to a good hotel, as if there was a past.

In 2010, her prince saved 16, L, from jumping in front of the train into the railway. He checked-in for his bypass, and she was sitting on the bench waiting for the train to arrive from a distance. It was all coincidence. They stepped in the same train wagon and met each other on the same couch. They sat against each other. L shouted her prince her name. He was like "Hello!?". They talked until the train stopped at their final destination. He had to go but she had to stay to travel further alone. She liked him the first moment they touched.

She wanted to become a stewardess in heart and soul. She thinks that her passion for this was much more blue than *Camiel Eurlings*. She believed she was waiting for him. She was waiting for him in her apartment in Acid New York outside Dorthrin Firegale. It took 15 minutes before her prince came. She said: "Come in." With her heart passionately full. Such as this cannot be forgotten. His precious smile and his insecurities. Both spend a whole night talking about all sorts of stuff and drinking wine. He kept on pouring her glass of wine and she loved it. It made both at the end of the evening feel attached to one another. Both talked about nothing all time, but it was something. He went like "Awhh" She asked him "do you feel what I feel" and he said "yes!". She asked him to kiss her, well. He kissed her and it took them two full hours non stop… She was so amazed by his kiss. He made her feel so incredibly horny. It was a rush. Or not? She actually wanted to fuck him that night, but she held her temptation. He did too, she guessed? He talked about the letters both wrote to each other and about the Swan Lake where she was the main character. It was history. It all seemed like a mythology. Yes. A mythology that only existed in her dreams and history. She prepared herself on the worse.

Her prince, her male cousin and her brother were sentenced to death. They were not allowed to play loud music in their neighborhood. Sixteen, L said: "go away!". Who is supposed to tell someone to decrease or lower the sound in their villa. They are the ones supposed to decide on their own whether they increase the sound of their sound systems.

Twenty years ago there used to be a foreigner. He came instantly whilst the family was having dinner. He yelled at 16 that she was not supposed to have someone else. Well, L was already taken and her family looked full wonder and surprisingly to the foreigner. We remembered that he had a lot to comment about our violations in the household that didn't exist. Sixteen and her family don't remember whether they kicked him out of the house or he just disappeared. He never returned and never came back. We all thought of the good in humanity. Yes. There is the chance to make the world a better place for all.

The day that the attack fell between 45 and 16, her prince changed into "goat cheese". What actually happened between the prince and forty-five and sixteen. There was something in the air. After L her prince and family fired the bombs there was some kind of peace in the air. It smelled delicious. In the neighbor they kept it quite unseen and they all stuck up their thumbs in the air. He was dead. Everyone in the world was talking about the accomplishments of L and her prince S. Well, they never spoke about it until the day she published it in the net. They screamed. They said at the end that she was right and correct and that ADELEW was mistaken. There was actually no space for triumphantly.

This happened to S and L in their younger years. By this time S was already cursed but his change would only take place after his hollow era after reaching his birth date age of 32. She had a terrible experience as a child at the age of 16. Later both decided when both would create children of their own to cherish them with all their heart and soul with the protection from harm by humans like 45. In the new planet of beasts and animals children played and mothers made dishes with food they had left. Yes. A somewhat animal life's. Beasty children. Protected by the love of wizardly and fairy creatures, animal birds and shrubbery trees and flowers.

Some beasts needed to be taken care off and needed to be measured and weighed to see if there was any chance of surviving between the humans. In the villages and fields of Dorthrin Firegale humans weren't part of their existence and were being left alone on their planet and there was no other ordinary changeling like L. Sometimes it took a while before another humanly change would occur by Lucifer. The sunrise was sparkling through the golden fields with magical glooming flowers and the horizon of the glittering ocean was everything what nobody could ever imagine with high tide. He, S wanted to leave L human. Both adored looking towards the stars in the galaxy and looked to the sky and played pattern games with them like *Memories*. Both would remember the points they see and both would hold another's hand to draw the guidance in the stars.

In Dorthrin Firegale village Superbia L enjoyed playing with her Halflings, their son and daughter, all loved the new world in Dorthrin Firegale. They would drink magical milk in the hope for them to grow and had a magic power to rise glowing flowers from death alongside their other powers as being fast, clever, ordinary and simply fantastic. Flanking with Trees they had magical powers in healing raped children like two by humans like 45 by guiding them through their mending. They could bravely leave a magically dreamy sign during their mystical occurrence. With the help from the Halflings makes them feel satisfied in their hearts. The Halflings lived from the moaning of such man and woman and the loving change in helping release those youngsters from pedophiles. While playing their enchanting instruments with musically magic sounds gave them even more power to rule and control their curse in aid. They had features from their mother L when she was still a civilian and the features of their father S as a leader. All where well-

mannered, incredible, excellent,
artistic, powerful and lively cursed.

Part 11

She returned at her studio apartment
from her stay at the "La Royal Smile
Hotel" and surprisingly both ex's
where vanished. It felt good. For some
past time after having followed him S,
on all the things started to come
closely and she wrote a letter to her
prince. In her bed she thought of him
and wished he would love her soul.
But she couldn't find his love. She
rises now and both traveled to other
cities, hanged around in streets, both
seeking each other or the one who
would truly love their cursed souls.
She looked at him that night, with
terrified eyes. She told him that she
was looking for the one, without
telling him, and that she didn't find
him yet. Love didn't envy. He was
being faintly and rude and told her he
was going to another country. He
didn't tell her when he would come
back. So she asked him if she could

kiss her. But the kiss was also dimly.
As if the love had faded. She believed
that two were better than one, because
it is a good reward for the two at the
ball. She told the prince when she
came to save her that she was alone
for two years and that she fell. There
was no one there to lift her up except
him. So they went to bed and had sex.
He laid her gently down in bed polite
and outrageously roughly taking his
clothes off. He played with her toy.
She was so surprised how experienced
he was. He really left her with her
eyes wide open. After she came
several times he penetrated her
deeply. She was extremely wet. Before
they entered the room she told him
that she was afraid of him and to
break again. So he told her to turn
around, and he made her come more
than 50 times. He came. Again, if the
two were together, they kept it warm.
He was devastated to pass her. She
loved him, and let him follow his

dreams, and later both introduced themselves, after the wedding, to their family's places. She and he spoke in the language of angels and demons, in Latin, without having to speak. They had the love. She was chaotic. If she only had the power to understanding his mysteries and knowledge, so as to move mountains like love can do. But she couldn't because she didn't have his magical powers, love and without love she just couldn't speak. She and her prince filled each other up with highly gifted language. They did not speak. They just showed each other the way. The love they had geared all things and endured everything. While dreaming and writing all this. About the things that have been accomplished after the wedding. It felt overwhelmed for some past time she and he have followed all things closely, to write a letter to each other.

In L her imprint by S she will always remember her wonders in her dreams. She remembers the hopes she had in meeting him once again after the incident with 45 when he came to save her. One day, maybe 2 or 3 years from now, maybe not. She can't even decipher the thought of her being in commitment. She is ready. Soon enough, jealousy won't matter because she has him. She wants him to meet her family. They will go on adventures together like skydiving, scuba diving, mountain climbing, and everything in between… Together like ice put beside a raging fire! She is probably in love before they will meet. But that's okay, because they intend to be the last partners in life, no matter how long it takes. She knew it was worth the wait! Sixteen, L and her prince S winked. There was work to be done. She knew that Lucifer had a better plan on when they would meet and get together. The train station, either by jumping in front of the train or waiting for the train to arrive.

To celebrate S and L their wedding in a beasty world, in Dorthrin Firegale it comes along with rides of claxons decorated in golden glooming flowers and animals running behind their creaturely rides. Their ways thanking the bride for catching the flower of the bride goes along with songs singing "Asante Sanaa" meaning thank you in *Swahili*.

Once a new sunset broke through Dorthrin Firegale after the festive winter wonderland wedding celebration in the deepest Forest on earth, the animals and beasts in the lightest fires of hell hallowing came alive. It didn't matter from which creed the wishes were. They all fought for a prayer in love, life, future and happiness and to overcome the curse by the demons time to suck and grasp the death in the under hells of the deepest fires when 3 tops got crossed.

Although death was written upon them in the civilian world, no human nor beast or animal not even the slightest shrubbery Dandelion ever spoke or whispered of S and L their fully name, although they new their full names. Some found it difficult to communicate with them through bilingualism. Some unwanted demons and others, humans, wanted to know their full name out of curiosity. Civilians, animals, beasts and flowers would always remember their daily routine... In Dorthrin Firegale they will always remember what S and L would do the first thing in the morning in the humanly planet at the age of 23, after nights with demons whenever they wanted to keep their thoughts off them with cocaine, they would numb their craving victory by healing it with more addictives like

Black Vodka, *Gin Bombay Tonic* or even stronger *Whiskey*. They would drown the adrenalin craving of cocaine and combine the kill with weed cigarettes to not feel the desire. Humans, birds, creatures and flowers all had their own magical way of saying thank you to L and S for their hard work in their daily human life or their secretly life as beasts. The most common one and the most remembering one is "*Asante Sanaa*" that was being whispered by the shrubbery Dandelions and animal Gentle-birds and Ladybirds. Demons and demonic humans aren't as thankful as a thankful whispering song as animals, creatures, shrubbery trees and flowers thank you song in Dorthrin Firegale because they feel everything in lyrical notes in how a magical beauty appreciates those words of thankfulness that can bring more enchantments alongside the evolving beauties of the magnificent beast. Straight from Heaven or Hell.

There is no cocaine, weed, XTC or other pill nor painkiller to ease the numb. Hell is the creepiest, strongest place to grief. When you see the bravery in a glowing golden flower or bird that loses its feathers. A beasty newborn in hell. there is nothing you want to do than just release them from their curse.

Magical Dandelion flowers find strength to give away their baby petals during their gloomy bloom with fire and to hide this from Lucifer. If Lucifer isn't on earth seeking for lost souls. Some are so young they can barely stand on their own. Some blow away and find the strength to remain alone. Some wolf children can read and write but there is no higher degree of school to accomplish their universities on earth. Some animal birds, eagle birds are really helpful and help with removing mad snakes falling and taking over the less bits in hell. Baby snakes. They are excellent, noble and sweet. Some want to be like S. The creatures in this world are fantastic. Living in a fearless world. With delight and precious thoughts. Everyone is well mannered and bloody smart or totally caring between severe worlds of madness! All those creatures except for some humans and demons are friends, and they surely do carry names that can be pronounced longer than just one letter. Every animal, creature and plant had a hollowing name and L and S remembered them dearly even in their afterlife. Those names were carried by them in all worlds to always be remembered and every animal, creature and plant had a magical name to always be remembered with belonging letters attached to their names longer than one letter. The names were easier to remember in Dorthrin Firegale than on earth.

The imprint of L and S lasts during nights and under the bright moon it is underneath his clothes where L finds the love of the one man and the boy she chooses to be with in outrages and politeness beasty love. She surrendered completely to his firm movement. He does her with his and she does him with hers. This goes on for hours until he does her and she does his. Sitting on his lap he grabs her with is manly big hands by her humps and controls her movement firmly back and forth. He lays her polite on her stomach so that he lies on top of her with his chest and moves inside her. He slides his chest on her back rubbing her ass. His lower tummy moves back and forth over her buttocks. He takes her from front to back and side to side in all silhouettes and corners of the room. Sometimes with one leg bent as he gropes her from the front. Her favorite position was when he takes her against the wall from behind. As he strokes her with his hand between her legs and touches her on that one spot where he circles and goes up and down with his fingers along with his masculine that goes in and out with every movement until both reach their moment. Sometimes in cuffs and in all colors. She likes it best in bed when he is on top of her taking control with his left hand and sometimes with his right hand until she comes in the moment. During Crown moon was the time to make love with each other like never before.

The bond made them feel more and more attracted to each other. Some connecting on their yacht by sunrise. Hitting in their new kitchen on their cooking island. Bonding when clothes in the dryer or washing machine. Coloring in their swimming pool and

Jacuzzi where both changed the water after different outrageous sex. They did it everywhere except in the sauna because it is difficult to clean and it colors too much. They had sex inside and outside the lines. They take their time and their sex usually lasted seasonally all night. The most exotic moments are the coloring outside the lines. In cuffs or not. With *"jeu de rôle"*. She is his "Bella" his *"Mi Bella"*.

Part 12

It reminded him as his first kiss. She was already written for dead by the eagle she held in her left arm, as a cursed lost soul, by a bite that led her to no newly born change but into a Halfling demonic *Estries de Adze Nachzehrer*. This gave her the power to poison her prince S during their date night but little did she know that he was a divine. It all happened at the dawn of the night. At night her demonic creatures came knocking and ringing at her door on the cursing 13th of the month. Every cursed thirteen of the night. They asked her to go out. When she lived alone they came at night on specific cursing times and one night she could remember that it would be her last night she would remember, and it would be her last night as a human. They came by two or more. The head of the pack and his followers. They where just like

Dracula. They were actually brothers of each other. They brought her to the woods deep down the forrest. She had fun with her demon friends without noticing they were actually demonic vampires. Until the thirteen of the day they bit her and she somewhat turned into them, it was the brother of the demon friend, and she turned into a demonic crime, criminal. His brother, of the head, didn't want it, but it happened, and it was already too late. She was a partial cursed divine with a toe tasting the darkest fires of hell.

She turned to one of them but not precisely. A demonic criminal with a criminal mind. They had sex with each other. She on top of him in the witness of his brother and he also wanted to join the French sex game. They were supposed to travel after the sex game and adventure. Where they would go, she had no clue. She was clueless. But she knew that before she would go on a journey with them, she would have to say goodbye to her family, especially her sister. Before they left, they committed a crime on a house on humans she cared about. They sucked the blood out of the civilians living in those houses and committed multiple attacks. They sucked the blood out of the people who lived there and they made sure they ran darn hard away. Those humans never survived the curse and ran dry. As soon as they had what they wanted, just before as they had what they wanted, they heard the sirens and the cops came. We slept during day light, and awakened at night. It was cursing midnight again. The time came to say goodbye to her worship family. She actually didn't want to become one of them and she disliked herself and mostly her curse. She went back to her family and delivered them her diamonds and gold. Her sister said "if you give me your precious ring, I will give you my necklace, and that special ring, well it is your lucky precious, so you don't need to give it to me. You may keep it for yourself. The ring querida, it is your curse to carry and withhold."

L gave her one wallet of the pack and told her while whispering in her ear that she should burn it. Her sister, she wondered why? She sensed something cursing affecting L. she told her sister that this was the best option to get rid of them. She told her family that she would never return and she said goodbye to the family. They went on their way to a speedboat that was of one of the demonic brothers. "Oh no!" said L. He smelled fire… He was on fire… He was looking for where the fire was started… He noticed that his wallet was stolen or away, and he went after the fire to redeem the fire while he was slowly solving. After he couldn't find his wallet, that L gave to her sister, he decided to take L and his brother as fast as possible into the speedboat while all three where on fire. L didn't care, because she didn't want to have this curse in the first place. Especially because she lost her family. She decided to jump off the boat into the water to decrease her pain. But they did it too. They didn't go away. Because of the water they recovered and she stayed a victim in crime. A demonic Halfling.

At night L experimented with her power by showing the qualities she was looking for in her next life, being specific and realistic. She pulled the paper and sprayed her blood, then fold it into an envelope and put it into a bottle. She held black rose petals in her hand while picturing her prince and would throw the bottle out of the boat and picture herself with him for eternity. She put the petals into the envelope and sealed it with a kiss of blood, demonic blood. With blood on her poisoning lips from the partly curse that needed one more demonic experience only.

"No" did not always mean "no" among her demon friends. In order to avoid conflict and maintain smooth, pleasant relations, she rarely said yes directly. "Yes" may have meant "maybe" or "I'll consider it." A negative reply was unlikely to be fulfilled. The "yes" she told them was actually a no, but was probably misunderstood.

She smiled to transfer kindness and goodwill. But the demonic friends who took her away with boat saw it as a gate to take her with them into crime. The expressions of L were maybe too smooth, but in her sight awkward or embarrassing if she wouldn't smile, which may appear inappropriate. The distance between her and her family became greater distance when talking about body language. She would never see them after the spell. The spell could only be undone if her prince would have received the bottle with her bleeding kiss stamped with the roses. Only if he would receive the bottle to burn it.

She started to feel her heart beat. She looked at her demonic friends in crime with a sparkling body and held her hand close to her heart. She went into salvation. She said: "it is good to have you sister, hold my hand, we will walk through this life together. Sister, it is good to have you sister, my soul, my heart, my protector, my shiny star for life." They where furious. She said: "Guys, it is too late". She went to heaven and back. It was like a journey through a traveling machine into space to survive from a coma. She thought she would never wake up and wanted to know what was behind that door. It was shining so bright. But the voices behind the door said: "No, not you. It's not your time yet. You shall go back and live again!".

The legends say that the burning of her heart stopped when going to Heaven or Hell, for them to go see a place of worship. The holy place would show the black and white shadows of their soul on Kodak film. The temples would speak of surgery and radiation preventing liquid death for tiny microbes that could be smelled in a Destinies Palm's temple. Only macro-life in here, bitches and nicotine. Poisons that cure. The place of worship owners had the means to let live or kill those who inflicted both should take the waves. The teddy bear under the *Eifel Tower* in Acid Paris was a warning.

The burning behind her eyes stopped when her heart was released from

them. S, the prince showed her, her
pure heart. The black and white
shadows of her soul, between his
morning coffee and his afternoon
guitar. He concentrated on the scent of
her burnt heart from the blood and
fire that made him waft off his white
coat while he was speaking. A sign
had gripped her tight and only her
senses that squeezed between the
fingers could take in what was left of
her. Her prince smelled the liquid
death. He received the bottle and
burnt it with a poison that cured L. He
had the power to kill those who
inflicted her change in a demonic
vampire and remain into an
enchanting magical change of a
fantastic and magnificent beast just
like S himself the emperor wolf in
Dorthrin Firegale.

She became "Free at last, free at last,
thank Hell almighty, free at last." Well
that is what they both thought. No

humanly man, no matter how many years he spent rotting in the halls of a shrine, can tell the future. ADELEW, 45, took the balance of her life away. It's a reminder, an exercise of an asshole with a degree and a demonic-pedophilic complex. But when L was sixteen, her prince gave her something. He gave her, her life back and made her heart full. Both were given a purpose.

The Crown-moon bath tube is hot and perfect as black rose peddles lay on the floor and Champaign is being poured on top of the L her shoulders

The ground started to rumble.

The star tops and bright moon are getting closer.

The wolf cries.

The beauty and the beast applied a poison after going together to bed and lived happily together for eternity between two worlds.

The two *Babylon lights* at last join for the artists together and all flame and thunder.

Part 13

The only beasts or animals on Earth
that can predict the future are artists.
They can see pictures that don't exist,
stories that haven't been told, and
technology that could never exist.
Religion, which had seen them
through all the years of their life, had
finally fallen short. It was similar to
the day when she and he realized
their parents were beasts, with
limitations and flaws. It changes
things. Both decided to change with
them. Both stopped sleeping. Why
bother? School was painted in the
snow. Both would be dead at the end
of the marathon with no medals.

Their story needed a friend not a
demon like Carmilla. The disease was
hard to personify. Really, it is just
both their own body betraying them.
The evil twin story like a Hollywood
blockbuster. No, both needed a fable
to justify the journey into hell or

heaven. Both keep dreaming about some one together couldn't see, steering their life along a path, past each milestone they never thought both could handle but still made the choice, rushing toward death. Both named this a faceless force. Together wanted to give their mother, the wanted whole *"Casey Jones"* practices, but instead she and he were screaming of their life to be a dress, suit and tie. Their ex's live and die by a schedule, the pocket watch never was ready. Both choose to become like their cursed demonic enemy, partners in crime like *Bonnys and Clyde*. They would die and go to hell or heaven. Both trimmed their hair and all history went away. He and she cleared out their studio apartment in Acid London on earth outside Dorthrin Firegale. Both made neat piles of their books and clothes. Each and every single book needed to be scheduled by height and arranged by color and piled closely by the edge. It was all gone in the morning. Both kept a bed and a suitcase in the middle of the floor near their bed, surrounded by every cursing clock they could set their hands and a calendar to remember when he and she want to kiss there brother and sister before they die. Both were going to die in six months from the minute the Destinies Palm's trees sang the last note. Both ignore their bills. Both their ex's used to ignore them, but still S and L still handle to pay alimentation for them. Their ex's wanted to press S and L back into their life, into society to die in a bed. Both spoke in commandments. Thou shalt not kill and save on toilet paper and make payment in 30 days. They were wrong. Both were off the grid, under the radar and running wild. S and L slipped away with amazing grace. The time spins amazing while both sit in a fevered trance, noticing the exact moments of the day. That day, when the day becomes an end. The end of humanity. Together sit in the couch and into the floor in a halo. The order of time doesn't matter, because together they are never going to assess it. He and she simply do not have the time for it. Both just need to scream it out loud, gauge the nail head with the hammer before the swing, no, cock the hammer before pulling the trigger. Both don't live in their studio anymore. It was their temporary shelter. Soon the demonic creatures will discover. In the past years S and L have been experimenting with hard drugs. Their nose now bleeds every single time. Both believed that one night their nose was bleeding in their sleep, they shockingly woke up and luckily their pillow was still white. It seems to be some kind of warning that both should quite cocaine. Both don't have enough time left. Both use a pencil to write one another special letters. Both do it every day with a black feather from one another's beloved one in red ink that arises with the blood Forsaken moon that has had a trip around their brains and is so easy to write with. Their heart knows what to say. It stops on Christmas Eve. The day before today L smiles when he, S, arrives at the door. The glooming mother flowery fairies take her back and she starts to dance ballet again with her sunken bones. It changed her shape again. They never asked if she wanted an ambulance. She choose to open a case and to invest some money into his hand instead of a ride to his 45-year-old holiness, if only because his death is not written down. He fades away with ease after the long wooden crate is dropped onto the floor. She opened the curtains for the first time since isolation and had been hurt by 45. Nobody suspects both L and S would become a butterfly with the one and only. Now both sleep, both shower, and both dress and wear make-up. She likes to dress herself up in the perfect dark blue suite that lay folded like a masterpiece in the walk in closet. Both used more cocaine than together have dared before. She was wearing her pumps without socks or stockings and went for work.

All four of the watches on their stand ring in concert. Time to apply the venom. Now it begins. Both were wearing leather coats that cost more than their first car. She and he bought the winter jackets two sizes too big and it is still too big. Both tried shaving everyday, but the ashen skin of both magical flower started to bleed even before the razor touched it, just like written. The flower was hastily Palm treeded by nail scissors, and the long gray hair was pulled back into a ponytail with a red scarf.

The two blocks to the station did not happen exactly as L and S planned. L and S called a taxi and the taxi hit the Audi at the third light. The cops came out of the coffee shop a second after L and S stood behind into the street in Hyacinth-Blossom-Street. L and S took a pee behind a car and before she knew the cops where standing there while the garbage truck rattled by. L and S moved under influence like a ghost, threading the thin line between death and alive. The metal of the hand coughs knobbed of L and S their bloody spine, and their thin legs where screaming to stop, but they raged on. Just like a star getting caught for OD. L and S their mouth were tucked up under their granted cheekbones. They were dressed in black with a pink originally scarf from Acid Paris and ringing for survival, sunken with stoned red eyes in the hood of Hyacinth-Blossom-Street. 45 put his fingers up in his ears for the

horns and waggled his tongue at L
and S. L and S kept on doing it with 45
while burning their gasses of their
chest, him pressing her into a rise of
pain. The old lady at the station
grasped and screeched "*el Diablo*" as
she scampered past. The cocaine rages
in L and S their veins, and their hearts
was going to burst.

All beasts, except one specie, survive
heartless. Once L and S were also
known in the name of a modern
wolves child. She was not a wolves
child that lived in nature and was
brought up by creatures and animals,
but a child that grew up in absolute
isolation as a result of a original and
unique bizarrely form of enchanted
child that was going to evolve into a
wolf. Shortly after the discovery there
were various investigations into her
development.

She was the fourth child and the
second alive child of unstable

somewhat animal beasty parents. Her mother has been somewhat blind and her father, who was twenty years older than her mother, was suffering from depression as a result of a car accident that took the life of L and S's mothers in their later years. When L and S were 20 months old and finally started to talk a little, a Palm tree told their parents that the girl showed that she was perhaps slightly coming from two worlds, literally meaning that she would show politeness, confidence, outrageously, original ideas, fantastic ideas and laziness in others development by a curse increasing her power of her third eye. Till now, the exact cause of her well manners has not yet been established. There was also a talk of a mental supremacy. There were many possible causes for creating the power such as hereditary, congenital, brain damage, and traumatic, non-congenital brain damage. A frequent cause is an oxygen deficiency during or immediately after birth. Well manners could be global or *Lucifer*, meaning that it is possible that such a person can work better than others in certain areas or within other worlds that only wizards knew about.

Since the father and mother felt that both were heavily clever and smart, they wanted to protect him and her without fully isolating them from the outside world. They decided to keep both in closed rooms. Their demonic creatures regularly abused them in their younger years. Abuse is usually not possible, but specially adapted education, such as available in Acid Amsterdam, and special needs of education provided in Brussels, or specific support in the ordinary education could be obtained in order to arrive at the maximum achievable level of development in their situation.

In practice, it was particularly important to assess to what extent L and S themselves, or children like L and S, could live independently, alone, or in a beasty pack and whether they needed regular or 24-hour guidance and support form animals, shrubbery or creatures. This would then include looking at all levels of personal care, social skills and emotional skills, in relation to the degree of ability. In the case of L and S, as a human. They were referred to as divinity children, S was a wolves' child and L as a wolf child would later transform into one and was inflicted to be one, both destiny to be wolves lovers. The wolves' child could be in a setting with accompanying of caring staff from mostly animal birds and trees. If the child would be on her own without ability to eat, talk, wash, dress or go to the toilet, there would be a big need for intensive care by animals, creatures and shrubberies. Many of these very serious children will only have difficulties learning to walk without the help of elves and wizards. A sleeping house or only for a few days per week. When L and S were 13 years and 7 months old, their blind mothers decided to leave their husbands. Both mothers went to an organization for demonic social workers supporting the blind, and there they took their children from them. The demon human social worker that saw L and S thought that both were 6 and 7 years old. After a short period of rehab both L and S came in a demon host family. Both went to special private schools. Both learned to have friendly animal, shrubbery and creature relationships including both with humans and demonic burglars and criminals in their surroundings, and eventually he and she learned how to talk and even sing. However, both would soon reach a ceiling in the level of their development. Religious beast Fathers and Mothers followed their development since they hoped to discover if language skills could develop in the teenage years. But the Destine Prophet Palm tree that saw L and S when they were 20 months years old was entirely wrong. Her magical bright order made that the results of the investigations always remained debatable. The mothers of L and S had, in the meantime, undergone treatment of their eyes and recovered by wonder a large part of their eyesight. At that time, L and S turned 18 years old now and decided to go back for a short time to their mothers, but when it became clear that the care for their son and daughter was too heavy for their mothers, and once again L and S their Halflings were placed in animal host families once they received a death note that both parents were dead after a trip to earth outside Dorthrin Firegale. Tree Nebulan world.

Before the marriage both lived in houses for adults in the south of Droplet Cloud. Her younger brother was also still alive. The love for her father and mother remained unchanged and beyond unconditionally from childhood to her adult years. She always realized that it took just as much from both parents, and wanted the happiness of both parents to not stand in the way. During this era L and S like someone who is a bit insane and comes from an elite place. L and S are of the opinion that their madly battle scars, rcsulted from wounds during the battle against 45, are outrageously sexy because it means that both saw the mess of madness, the truth is that both find love in their silly life and both keep that feeling in the human world and beyond.

L and S, they preferred death upon 45 more than that they had to sit trapped. It is really simple and not unusual. L made herself look fantastically original and outrageously with this idea. Afraid of some humanly perception about her. It is her wild and rebel side without reason. Death in Heaven and Hell. There is something about death that is reassuring, as she wants the change so much. The silence in the days it helps. She learned that now! In the afterlife she cherishes all the little things with all her might and soulless heart. Appreciating the life more till the change into her beasty life's to the utmost. It doesn't matter where she is, between humanity, animals or beasts, everywhere she is she sees herself always stargazing outside with her nose towards Earth sky wishing that she could travel somewhere else. L and S were struggling with uncertainty, but in remembering these uncertainties are times that everyone has in their life when heading towards a foremost spectacular event in their lives, the marriage. She believed there was so much wrong with her, really incredible. In reality she was an original beautiful enchanted princess and she was to become and change into a divine beauty queen.

As soon as she found her prince S on his white horse both will together take the step to the legendary wedding. After climbing out of bed both feel most sexy. He has tattoos and she has second hand clothes, but there are also other sides of her that made L and S who they are now. Frankly they love everything from boys and girls with bizarreness. And both fathers, well they are great artists and one of them is a great pianist but they have always believed he was a greater father to them. Yes. The best father of the entire world. Both choose to be bizarreness to be towards their demonic creatures. Their demonic creatures saw S and L as delusional boy and girl possessed by evil. But because of the emerging episode of *digital media*, both could tell that there was a chance that both weren't that delusional at all. Both were victims of electronic harassment. The electronic harassment involved directly to energy weapons such as computer hacking, and other violence that involves electronics. The opponents could access their security alarm television, clock, cell phone and computer. They accessed anything electronics. They changed the display dates and clocks on L and S her electronic devices. It simply happened. Listening, however, is something she consciously chose to do. Their voices were not their shared thoughts, and she ignored the bad voices. It was good for L and S to not listen and not anticipate to the suicidal voices. She gave them attention in earlier episodes, but once they appeared in other era's she decided to ignore them. In the past, they played with her emotion, and they used a possible magic imaginable medium. They were opponents of the past.

L and S are adventurers with sensations for children beasts, creatures, plants and flowers, animals particularly the tigers and lions that appeared in Oculus Star Way that nowadays let them cold. Both share thousand dreams with one to never be alone. Both belong to one another. Magically Waiting. Waiting for days to turn into nights, days turn into weeks. Weeks to turn into months before S and L have a wedding in virginal white, in the church, traveling to their winter wonderland in the deepest en darkest grounds in the forest on earth for the animals and creatures and shrubberies to be able to attend alongside humanly friends and

to live a happy life in their castle.
Some days, weeks and months
suddenly seem much longer, and
perfect nails seem rather useless by
craving. Both feel comfortable with
undressing and dressing in the
shower. To surprise…

She would like to surprise, the one,
him with her castle. Both have money
now to buy a little palace for four, but
both just rent a studio in Acid
London. He could be as good as a
prince as L her father was for her.
They would live a longer life than
Babylon Candles. Their love was
something from above both could
barely see but had to feel. A love out
of time and mature. A love that was
divine. A love that she could hold and
keep.

The watches all beep again, 1 minute
to go.

The beginning of the Dragon Elves is just up ahead.

The bath tube is cold and perfect as it perches on top of their shoulder.

The ground starts to rumble. They kneel on behalf of *Jesus Christ*. The stars and moon are getting closer. The horn sounds. The Beast is panicked. Their noses start to bleed, both smell the gas.

She grabs a bullet and pulls the trigger like bitter Russian roulette. He applies the venom.

The tube of water in the bathroom keeps pouring. The gas burns their face.

The two lights at last join together like Babylon lights and all in all it is flame and thunder.

Both smile now as eternal royal leader husband wolf and queen wife divine…

In the new planet both were raising their Halflings. Both were delighted. Lucifer and Medusa wanted to see their newborns. All were happy and enchanted by the gifts sent directly from heaven and hell. Gifted children mingled with earth, wind, water and fire. Both L and S still planned voyages to humanity and left the animal world for the Halflings to understand where their mother L originally originated. They were 85 percent divine but consisted for 15 percent of human blood after all. Although they liked birds and trees more over civilians. L and S enjoyed reading their Halflings stories before bedtime. Dressing them into the most masterpiece clothing. Life was different on both planets. Nevertheless, none of them argued and both worked hard to keep the family together with no divorce. Let alone finding one another in the arms of another beast or human. This did not occur and wasn't going to happen.

Part 14

After the two lights joined, arisen
from the venom they both applied
when being together. Both once knew
that they had to make one last voyage
to show their children's, their
Halflings the life of humans in
demonic world continents. To
safeguard their Halflings paths they
decided to travel both once more.
They had their leather suitcase packed
for their Halflings incase something
would happen during their voyage to
this part of earth. Everything was
arranged for daughter and son. It was
a continent well known that of
dangerous burglars and vamps,
demons. Their final trip would be to
the Tree Nebulan world. He was
already there before she got dressed in
suite to get ready for the impossible
delegation. She was as pale as a half
toned skinned after all. Both arrived in
Tree Nebula world. Demonic burglars

that wanted them to pay in hard drugs and gold surrounded them. Pay for their yacht filled with white and blue diamonds and cash money. In the meanwhile S was seeing a demonic criminal for gun weapons. In return for he offered their private jet to be safe… L didn't have a clue of the deal and S didn't tell L about this deal with the demon. It happens to be their ride back. Little did both know they got offered a demonic shrubbery soup with the name mushy-roomy. After a couple of hours all of a sudden the stars seemed to be floating like boats. The walls started coming closer and the clocks turned into beasty baby faces coming closer and envisioned by the mother of the Lord *Jesus Christ*. Mother Maria. Heaven.

A wolf friend that lived among the civilians happened to be one legged in his animal and humanly form. He once crossed a firebomb field once to be found in world war 2 in waters that was dangerous for all creatures either human or beast or animals of the sea. He crossed the water fields filled with atomic bombs to help his lost son who accidently fell in the waters and couldn't swim. He would never forget the sound of the first "beep". After hearing this, his life was sentenced to death. At least, that is what he thought. He was lucky he only lost one leg in his humanly form that later resulted into a damage of one leg in his beasty wolverine form. He thought he was going to explode in front of the eyes of his only son. It could have been his son or him. His mind went insane. He though of changing into a wolf in front of the eyes of humans sight seen on land and by using his power of speed to release its humanly formed leg from the atomic bomb. Luckily it wasn't his time to say goodbye to both worlds. He was one of the lucky ones to just lose one leg.

Tree Nebula world, is a land with a different sparkling and astonishing landscape. Both fantastic divines traveled towards the belonging horizon of the waters. It was like "The heart of Oculus Star Way" in a fairytale. In Tree Nebula world everybody lives in horror. The youth humans were being thought how to plunder and fight with gun weapons. Factories were replacing working children for their parents because of cheaper working hours. Women were making promises towards dead husbands and were forced to make love to their dead husbands. It was all terror brought by demons on those lands.

In this horrific world animal children's were forced to play with demonic fireballs. No adult was allowed to interfere and help the children creatures to read and write that were barely 1-year-old and to learn how to play with lyrical wind, air and water. Mothers got instantly killed who replaced the fireballs by the other elements of earth to learn their child to play with kind natural basics. The children on this part of the planet were instantly cursed children of the darkest era of hell in the civilian world.

Worries arose in the charmed love between L and S. Her husband had untouched. He unwavering chose to move alone. Little did he know that L would follow him wherever he would go. No animal, plant or beast knew how long he or she would be apart, nobody knew, they had no idea. Before saying goodbye they made fantastic polite love to one another. It wasn't outrageous sex anymore. This was also the time when both shared the same shower under the waterfalls after the bath. They were absolutely madly lovingly about each other. They made even more magical touched love. Before the night of Crown moon when she got changed and pregnant with carrying his twin children. With the time they had to say goodbye to their enchanting Halflings. Preciously imprinted forever theirs.

Their shared imprint and venom cursed them both to be absolutely insane about one another. Both couldn't stop biting each other. Both were always on each others eyes. Both carried each others love in their lively lost magical hearts and clever minds. She was always on his special splendid mind. He was in her every beat of her heartless soul. Both think that the love they giftedly gave one another was always more than just enough. It was bloody heartless but fully blooded by forsaken moon. They would instantly kill everyone who interferes with their love, their children and their family. They would change every family member that would lay in their death path to join them in their afterlife and release their secret. The magical world as a beast and other enchanting animals and so on… Their children awaken by crying when they were young and silenced for a bit once they received their magical milk…

Before L knew about S his secret of his magical divine during her magnificent international flight of which humans thought it was her suicide. Her imprint goes beyond and lovingly unconditionally before her change and trips with him, when they were together with the slow dance during the wedding before the change. Every single morning during the spring months she woke up and wondered if S would be alright. She had been thinking of his question to create little beasty creatures with him. She remembers wanting to tell him that he is the only one boy and the only man to become the father of their children. If everything is cool and both are doing alright. She can still remember dearly wanting to dream of their first kiss. Also the French kiss on the dance floor. A kiss that would last longer than one hour. A kiss that lead them to their first night. Both made imprinting love to one another during one if the many magical nights that they accompanied themselves. But his fantastic kiss. After his kiss she felt the imprinting spell… His imprint… with him on top of her… with her under him… both made love to one another… all night long… it happened at last during their Crown moon in the most expensive hotels in "Bora Bora". Room service was served by a demon friendly vamp and available that night… the relationship was over between both ex's both stayed together for a very long time with their ex's to finally let go and let their love life boundless for true love… The gemstones where returned and given as accessories to both lovers.

Lucifer promised that if S wanted to be free from his curse and his bitten ones including L and his Halflings, to live life again as a heavenly human, he would have to travel in time to protect L against the deed 45 and others did before they get hold of her and shouldn't leave L for a split second. S didn't want to reverse his curse and that of L and his Halflings. They actually started to like their powers. They turned into Angels from Hell. The only curse that could kill S and make him go to heaven is a golden bullet straight through his lovingly beating heart while he is part of Hell originating from Dorthrin Firegale, Superbia.

Lucifer and Medusa promised both belonged together with their beasty family. Reunited. It was time to tell rulers of hell that they no longer wanted to hurt them with the curse in whichever way hell looks at their love life.

As angels from Hell, both kept kissing each other, while both had freely magical blue tears in their eyes. They assumed that their original power above Lucifer and Medusa was a one-night stand. Still they kept trying to impress underdogs with their outrageously power. Both crushed all the animals their dreams. The Halflings seemed so strong sometimes, as a little girl who signs like a Swan and a little boy who Whizz's. Both showed one another all the best of themselves, both their best, it was fantastic, at least the way both wanted themselves to be magically seen and loved by hell and both felt like special beasts in the world Dorthrin Firegale. Proud. L was the lover of a man who's father was Lucifer and turned his son into an Angel from Hell in one night. She cried like a woman with a beating heart. He was worth all those tears that won't go away…

Back in Droplet Cloud in 2012. After her international flight in humanly form as can be L broke up with her ex as did S with his fiancée. During this period both met willing Gentle-birds and Gentle-men creatures, and Catalaya and Sunflower shrubberies in their human form to take care of her Halflings. This is the way L wanted for the best for their children to live among parents of which she knew they would give her son and daughter all the love they needed without to many human interference and demonic misleading.

As a beast they had family reunions too with a self home made chocolate cake from humanly Bruce in "*Matilda*". It was with glooming flowery candles enough as L's age to celebrate her birthday with her son and daughter singing en playing joyful and happy melodies together on the piano and guitar made by the birds. All creatures, animals and shrubbery, plants sang and played. It was one darn festive song. L found this lovely, lovely playing, and lovely cake both as lovely as one another. Beasts told her to not to forget to make a wish. And she prayed wished one darn magical spell upon the future of her Halflings.

Both had to attend funerals of family members in the civilized world. After playing her guitar and her piano often, wearing a dress especially her blue one. This time it was as dark as her unhappiness in this current situation she was in, she sat next to the bed of their son and daughter and read them a goodnight story. "The wedding was a malevolent event, everyone attended, the animals of the forest, beasts from the earth and sea, the elves formed water and fire, and there were tears of joy and songs of sadness and happiness, future, life, love, and the enchanted beasts and the beauties lived happily ever after."

She knew it was worth fighting for the love of S for when she looked at their son and daughter their playfully game of running away from water in dust, there is something more to life, something greater than Hell or Heaven, to that world they held on to that there is more than hope. In that opportunity of life, she could see clearly now that there was nothing to fear to the world they held on to in their afterlife. Except for the death upon their families that never changed or transformed into their world.

Before their trip to Nebula Tree world they kissed their only Halfling son and Halfling daughter goodbye. There was another errand sent from *Medusa* and *Lucifer*. Both had a feeling that this might have been their last kiss goodbye. They left a note for the owl bird nanny's and palm tree Destiny Prophet trees, who happened to be their only champion. The note was to make things easier every time they left to the civilized world. They told the champions that they would be back by Friday before spring.

In this new world there was one darn beautiful landscape, many divine deaths and easily for humans familiar with the known setting traps for us, wolves, to disappear in these fields of atomic bombs.

This was the moment for both L and S to start writing letters and notes to their children. Incase both would disappear and get trapped in a field set by demons and demonic humans filled with destroyable atomic firebombs for beasts too. They could be lucky but luck could also leave their side and circle 360 degrees the other way. They could vanish into dust and never be found.

Both would risk so much for their children and their love. If S would die, he is dead. She is willing to risk her life for love. Her life for his in turn of her own life.

Only 9 miles away from here they would arrive at their job for change. It was a trap! There where atomic bombs everywhere. Bombs and guns shooting. Both needed to get out! Their first light flashy thoughts went to their Halflings that they're safe with their animals and trees and that

they need a beasty mother and a
father to raise them. They had to come
alive together out of these fields.

Both traveled through the landscape.
Both traveled through water and wind
to find earth under their bare feet. Fire
was up ahead. Both were being
followed by cars with demonic
humans shooting, they were fast but L
and S were faster. Fast enough to
avoid those demon civilians from
harming them. Maybe rape and kill.
Maybe just kill.

They Kissed in early Spring.

Both run away.

Holding ones hands while crossing
the fields. Together rush through land
and sea. They lost touch through the
rough ocean.

She heard a "beep"

He kept telling L to rush while she wanted to let it go. She searched for a replacement. She stood still while she told him to stay. She couldn't move. She just couldn't possibly listen to him.

And she stepped away…

She was unluckily the one

S, he grabbed a golden bullet and pulled the trigger. Straight through his heart. His memory went mad. Both forsaken falling imprint will always be remembering that one night at the Crown moon bathtub that was hot and perfect as black rose peddles lay on the floor and Champaign being poured on top of their shoulders. The rumbling ground. The closer coming stars and moon. The crying of their cursed sounds as wolverines. The night of the change when she was a beauty and the beast applying the venom after going to bed together and lively make outrageous love to one another together for eternity. All in flame and thunder. No more *watchers* from hell in Dorthrin Firegale. Both now smile eternally as angels in heaven…

The end… 666

TO BE CONTINUED! PART 999

Part 999

Free at last. Heavenly stairs towards a door enlightened entrance walked with both dearly devoted loves hand in hand. Both stood perfectly and well mannered in front of the gate of heaven. Both were addicted to the way they touched. Both wanted to always stay close, in hell or heaven on earth. Close to their hearts without letting go of their hands. They are each other's greatest love. They both knew right away after cruising the highway that night with no breaks. The past weeks of autumn, the last days together went without limit. The love between them was that strong. They never left one another. Not even one split second. He'll be with her and she'll be with him. Both wish to tell to wait for one another to pass the gate. She wonders if he will tempt her into a black swan, love her forever in white and the need to share blessing moments in happiness and unhappiness for the rest of their life in heaven. Will his answer be yes? He is her unconditional love beyond earth and hell, and she knew it in this instant moment, the last time they met and went outrageously wild. She doesn't want anyone else above him. He gave her one last longing and eternal kiss in heaven with her *bordeaux red* lips in the early sunrise. Watching over their beloved twins on mother earth and beyond.

Both grip each other tightly by their hearts in heaven. Will you take her as your wife for the judgment of God? Said the Lord. Let God answer thou prayers… Both whispered one more time that both would never leave one another.

Both are extravagant angels in heaven as soon as both are on stage in heaven. Both are angels in bed, when he is on stage fine-tuning the equipment of his guitar on stage and she the piano on wings, the arena made in heaven. Extra clouds and angels as both play heavenly as both are working, on stage. As soon as both lays on cloudy beds both casts a spell on with their enchanting bodies on *Skype*, both are so beautiful both casts miracle spells on each other. Both have seen the paranormal moon at night, so close. Their high-strung reflections to love and more, the troubles of the world that both will enter with adventures endings in heaven, but above all ensure that both live a long and happy life watching over their charmed Halflings coming from both worlds.

Would you make her your wife in Black and White? Asked the Lord. Both don't want anyone else above. Both didn't have to say goodbye. It was clear that this woman really loves S, can S ever love this girl? A foolish princess who comes from a small

town about to be rescued by a beasty
prince. Because she still loves him
when she wakes up. How it hurts not
to have him in her life when she wants
to be his wife in pink and blue. When
she wakes she daydreams about the
way both met when she was eight, the
way both played memories, the way
both kissed. He has charmingly
enchanted her in every way and he
always brings a smile to her, even
when she is miserable. She wants the
world to see him and her together.
Forever theirs. Let them talk and
speak of them as legendary divine
lovers. I love you, you draw perfectly
in my dreams. Her body feels
different things in a thousand worlds.
Together they are complete, eager
loyalties. She wants to be his heavenly
wife, his queen in heaven and his
angel in bed, his love. She has
something to say to him that can't be
expressed in words, but in million
little pieces of her heart that is all

about him written in the patterns of the stars once shown by his own hands… all she wants is him… all she wishes is him… all she truly believes in… all she ever loves… him, dearly beloved S

In heaven. L planned to arrive late at the dining table of the Lord. Heavens gate is never closed but slightly open. Once L decides to enter, she directly gazes into S his eyes. She walks towards him on heavenly clouds and she feels her skin turn into trills of pleasure. They don't talk to each other, so she gives S a kiss that he directly rejoins with a tongue. She feels light shivers, because for this moment she was wearing her special lingerie. "Feel me, under my dress my love" she whispers. He glides his warm hands under her dress and directly touches hers. His hands stop for a bit. "Jezus, what sexy", he whispers sighing in her ear. He pushes her hard on a cloud and pulls her dress up, almost undressing her. Immediately she felt his warm soft tongue on her cross. L loses herself in his movements, that are slow but well thought and firm. While he turns L around on two knees, she turns herself and gives S a kiss. He rips off her dress while the material scuffs over her skin. She kicks of her heavenly pumps. He stands in front of her and she caresses his. She is tremendously wet once he enters a finger inside of her. "Stay low", he commands L. His tongue make circles. She looks up with a gaze that stayed hooked in his brown eyes. L hooks her hands in his brown curls and she lays herself gratifying on her back. Her idleness makes room for impatience. She wants to feel him inside of her. Now. Also S his patience is lost. He presses her on a bed of clouds and hits at once. His penis deep inside of L, his penis almost out of her. She looks into his deep brown eyes and she sees how sexy he is. Even S, he feels it while he keeps moving up and down, he grabs L her ass with his two manly hands. He squeezes firmly in her ass while he goes up and down. L loses her breath and feels fulfilled. He hits her once more and fills her with a moan with his sperm in L.

The accident in the civilized world led to his suicide and her death. Their skeleton was lost but their souls remained among creatures, shrubberies and beasts dreams and L and S became a vision in the clouds but their skeleton shall not lay under the earth. They were in the fires of hell and now belonged in the clouds of heaven. On earth, visions appeared in the dying fire at the fireplace. Their souls whispered in the glooming grasses of Dorthrin Firegale that wept once more that their souls was delivered in lightened places reaching for the darkness and light. They appeared hiding in the whimpering rocks. Trees would guide their Halflings lost soul out of the forest, the open door of their rooms would invite their parents soul into the light in their houses. L and S were dead on a flaming agreement but not dead cremated or buried. Those who are dead with no body buried or cremated are never gone. Their imprints would live. Their Halflings soul shall survive the flames of Lucifer by the power of their parents innocence.

A simple prayer. Their Halflings would travel through both worlds and soldiers of darkened shadows on earth from hell. Demonic creatures that rest in the darkest fires of hell took many lives since L and S disappeared. Loved ones who are dead with or without lost bodies are never gone. They are there in the thickening heavenly clouds. This double death couldn't rest beneath the earth. Both, L and S imprinted towards the heavenly trees in the civilized world that rustles. Both in the wood that groans. They become visible in the waters that sleep. L and S, their heavenly souls are among the people in the crowd. The rise of the vampires trapped humans like an pandemic in tall grasses that makes them lost as bate. Fire rocks are wolves only guidance to return the vampires to their dust, humans being trapped by meat eating giants deep in the forest where their cabin lives. Halflings use trees to protect themselves from losing ground, using water from escaping lands to poison the giants and make them *high*, wolves seek wood for lightning a flame for distraction of humans and children from vampires and pedophiles. Beastly, creaturely humans, shrubbery prisoners in hell as lost souls and Halflings yearning for deaths weeping silence in the darkest fires of hell. Wolves crying for another innocent soul lost by a pedophile or vampire. L's double death was an accident or destiny. The Halflings caught the wondering child souls around cross roads. It was a tragic kill with no body found on earth nor in hell.

Families in the civilized world had hope. The Halflings were to young to understand the death of their parents in Dorthrin. The ambulance, police, firemen and helicopters quite the search after some time and the black rose peddles vanished in silence as the tears of the Halflings stopped after decades once their parents souls became perceptible in their dreamy imprints and clouds. It was a matter of time for the twins to develop such skills. "Our mist… leave tonight's dream with a promise that the heart of our children rest silence, we'll wait for so many years and our tears await to know if our children's souls will come at light after many years."

The enemies of L and S in both worlds, the civilized world and dooming hell arranged some roses in all colors, partied with bottles of champagne and mirrors. Mirror's with lines of white powder, pulling needles and filled it with heroine and crawled to go to sleep again in silence in hell. The police sirens is the last thing they heard.

The END… 6-9

Acknowledgement

Herewith please accept my blissful thankfulness and recognition that shall never be of same importance as thou eloquence and thou devotion to write in thou name because, the succession is at first to thank by thou. Through dine dazzling loving gratefulness the unforeseen expert came by. One more, here is my gratitude, too petite, for though dedication and confidence.

A thousand kisses and thanks to my special and loyal family and friends, who have always been ready, finally, I want to thank the many other people. People who loved me through this book, especially those who talked about the things they read. Thank you for the assistant in the creation and design.

~ From Marlies van den Broek with Love

Biography

Marlies van den Broek, M.B van den Broek (born in Kenya; December 1986) is a Sagittarius and was a former ballerina who rose to worldwide fame as a writer. She practiced dancing at the age of 5 until the age of 22 years in many dancing disciplines and won competition prizes on top 3 rankings of every given contest. She grew up nearby Stone Town in Zanzibar and was raised spending most of her time in Rock City and Dar es Salaam. Her after school activities was going to ballet and during holidays she would travel through the Serengeti. Once her parents decided to make the big move to Europe, she continued dancing in more disciplines than ballet and swimming only. Her parents loved to travel. This added to the development of her to travel as well to countries within Europe. She was very sporty and practiced severe water sports rather than winter sports. She graduated from University and had a successful career within an American company in the Aerospace and Military industry situated in Miami. Her last ballet performance was in 2012 and this was the last dance saved with the time to quit, to change and focus on a different discipline. She has lived a part of her life in Paris. In Paris is where it all started and she received a contract to release her writings. She is an author of her favorites consisting of poetry "Love, Life, Future and Happiness" and romance fiction book "Beyond Unconditional Love" and thenfollowing "Unconditional Secrets Beyond Love, the first book is the most successful and critical book of popular books in the top 10 of best romance fiction. She has followers all around the world with focus in the USA and Canada. Overall the public wanted more of this book "Beyond Unconditional Love". This is the reason she has been working on a new book as a follow up "Unconditional Secrets Beyond Love". It is a wonder that Marlies could still write, this is precisely the egg from which the white swam emerged. Talent is of course in explicable. One either has it or one doesn't. but whoever wants to do something with it finds himself, to his surprise, more supported by his virtues than by his bad qualities. With her ideas she was also far ahead of her time. Concentration and the scientific humility to climb the highest mountain of her ladders time and time again. This enabled her to start writing a following to this book "Beyond Unconditional Love", which has been preserved from her to start with: the adventures of the children of L and S, and she created imperishable figures. Where she had broken her leg everywhere, the exaggeration. She could finally be herself. Without any concession to credibility, she put another new book in the world that is entirely hers. She is a madly gifted person in society. The question of who wrote both books has been solved. But even here some complications arise. "I got a pair of new pumps which I used to decorate the cover of my first and second book, although worn a few times."